HEART

My heart was po...
knew just who I w...
Finding a pay phone, I dropped in a qua...
dialed.

The phone rang and Steve's mother answered it. "Oh, Michelle, he's been gone since early this morning. He went shopping for some things for his ski trip, and then he said he was going to a meeting at Heather's house. Shall I tell him to call you when he comes home?"

"No, that's all right," I replied. "In fact, you don't even need to tell him I called."

I hung up the receiver and began to walk to the bus stop. Somehow the thrill of getting my job didn't last long knowing that Steve was with Heather. I wondered if anyone else had been at their meeting. After all, Heather had been Steve's girlfriend, and she had been the one to dump him. She was one of the cutest girls in school, and she obviously wanted Steve back. How could I compete with her when the two of them were just about to spend ten days together skiing in one of the most romantic spots in the world?

Bantam Sweet Dreams Romances
Ask your bookseller for the books you have missed

Hearts Don't Lie

Terri Fields

BANTAM BOOKS
TORONTO • NEW YORK • LONDON • SYDNEY • AUCKLAND

RL 6, IL age 11 and up

HEARTS DON'T LIE
A Bantam Book / February 1986
Reprinted 1986

Sweet Dreams and its associated logo are trademarks of Bantam Books, Inc. Registered in U.S. Patent and Trademark Office and elsewhere.

Cover photo by Pat Hill

ISBN 0-553-25367-0

Published simultaneously in the United States and Canada

Bantam Books are published by Bantam Books, Inc. Its trademark, consisting of the words "Bantam Books" and the portrayal of a rooster, is registered in U.S. Patent and Trademark Office and in other countries. Marca Registrada. Bantam Books, Inc., 666 Fifth Avenue, New York, New York 10103.

Printed and bound in Great Britain by Hunt Barnard Printing Ltd.

O   0 9 8 7 6 5 4 3 2 1

To Nanny, with love

Chapter One

How could I pretend to be thrilled with what Steve was telling me when he was breaking my heart? Sitting next to him in a coffee-shop booth, I wrapped my hands tightly around my cup of hot chocolate, suddenly aware that it tasted very bitter, and forced a smile as Steve continued to talk. "Can you believe it? My grandmother has to be the most incredible person in the whole world." He took a big sip of his hot chocolate, and his sapphire blue eyes gleamed brightly. "When she was here for Thanksgiving, she saw all the information the ski club had sent me about the Christmas ski vacation in Vail. I told her I'd give my right arm to go but that I hadn't been able to save enough money. Anyway, we talked about how much I loved skiing and how she used to ski herself and that was that. I didn't think much more about it. Then today, this came in the mail."

Though he'd already told me about the contents of the letter, he produced it for me to read. I took it from him and read his grandmother's neat blue writing. She said she was enclosing a check that should cover the amount he was short for the trip as well as some extra for spending money. It was her Christmas present to her favorite grandson, and all she wanted in return was for him to go and have a terrific time.

That was exactly what I didn't want. I'd seen the brochures that the Washington High Ski Club had sent home, too. They showed pictures of couples skiing down breathtaking slopes, pictures of couples snuggling in front of big fires in the ski lodge. It all looked so wonderfully romantic that I'd asked my parents if I could go, and I didn't even know how to ski. I had figured I could learn; I had done some waterskiing back in Arizona, where we used to live, and snow skiing couldn't be that much different, I decided. Besides, the thought of spending all that time with Steve in a winter wonderland made my skin absolutely tingle. Of course, my parents had flatly rejected the idea. Then Steve had decided he couldn't afford to go either, and I forgot about the whole thing. Good old Denver might not have the romance of a ski vacation in Vail, but it would be good enough for Steve and me as long as we could be together.

"How many times are you going to read that?" Steve looked at me quizzically. I realized that I'd

2

been lost in my thoughts and was still holding his grandmother's letter.

"Gee, Steve," I said, handing the letter back to him and hoping I sounded halfway enthusiastic, "your grandmother sounds like a wonderful lady."

Steve moved closer to me in the booth and slid his arm around my shoulders. "She's not the only woman in my life who's special."

I blushed and allowed my head to rest on his shoulder. From the first moment I'd seen Steve, I'd been glad I had had to move. His dark, curly hair complemented his gorgeous blue eyes. And although I'm almost five feet eight, Steve's six-foot build made me feel almost petite.

When I'd first transferred to Washington High, I almost didn't want to get to know him, in case his personality wasn't up to his looks. Then he had started sitting in front of me in history and behind me in English, and it wasn't long before I knew that his sense of humor, intelligence, and kindness were equal to his looks.

A waitress came over to our table, interrupting my reverie. "Can I get you anything else?"

"Yeah, I'll have another hot chocolate with lots of whipped cream!" Steve looked at me. "You've barely touched yours. Better drink up, it's cold out there tonight." Then he was back to the ski trip. He raved on about certain slopes and how huge he'd heard the moguls were on Devil's Run.

Then he started in on his equipment and how he wished he could buy some new bindings.

The waitress brought Steve's second cup of hot chocolate and set it down. She must have made him lose his train of thought because he quit talking and looked up. Then he waved to two people he noticed just entering the coffee shop. It was Heather Lance and one of her cheerleader friends.

They were exactly what I didn't need that night. The evening had already been depressing enough, and I hoped they'd just wave back and go to another table. No such luck. They walked over to us. Heather's greeting to Steve absolutely dripped charm, but she was barely civil to me. *Oh, well*, I thought. *At least she'll be gone in a minute.*

But Heather and her friend didn't leave. "Sit down," Steve offered. "If you've got time, I'll buy you a cup of hot chocolate. Hey, did you get the message that I called?" he went on. "I'm going on the ski trip!"

The other girl mumbled something about meeting some friends and left for another table. Heather said she'd be there in a few minutes and then sat down directly across from Steve. She locked her green eyes into his. Running her long coral nails lazily through her wavy long blond hair, she said, "I got your message. In fact, my mom said hearing your voice reminded her of old times. Oh, Steve," she said enthusiastically, "I

4

can't tell you how glad I am that there was a cancellation so you can go on the ski trip. I promise you're going to love it." She flashed him one of her perfect cheerleader smiles, and I wondered if he was even aware of me.

Heather, the president of the ski club, had been in charge of organizing the Vail trip. But I was positive that everyone who'd signed up wasn't getting the enthusiastic, personalized attention that Steve was. Suddenly Steve took his arm from around my shoulders. *He's interested in her again*, a part of me thought. *Not necessarily so*, another part answered. *He was only telling Heather something about measuring skis, and he couldn't do it with just one hand.* But then I panicked again. He didn't put his arm back around me when he had finished.

I sighed, wishing we could just get out of the coffee shop. I couldn't even think clearly with Heather around. She was competition that no girl needed. She was the school's head cheerleader, the original rah-rah golden girl. Her smile belonged in a toothpaste ad, and her long golden hair swung perfectly as she walked. She looked as sweet as the angel on top of a Christmas tree. But there were many who knew that beneath that angelic exterior was a very scheming personality. Heather was used to getting whatever she wanted, and she didn't worry much about who got hurt along the way.

She and Steve had been an item most of their

sophomore year. In fact, from what I'd been told, they'd just broken up a few weeks before I transferred to Washington at the start of our junior year. I stared at the two of them, sure that they were so involved in talking about skiing that they wouldn't even notice me. I had to admit that they made a gorgeous couple, the kind that photographers always show when they want you to buy prom pictures. Suddenly I felt very ugly sitting there with the two of them. Although my mother said I'd grown into a "lovely young woman," I still thought of myself as the girl who'd been nicknamed the giraffe in elementary school. Thank heaven I'd stopped growing and my friends had finally gotten taller. My braces had given me a nice smile, and a little eye shadow highlighted my blue eyes and my delicate coloring, but I was never going to be bouncy or bubbly cute like Heather. I stared at her long golden hair and instinctively put a hand to my own short, dark locks. What boy in his right mind would have trouble making a choice between us?

Rumor had it that Heather had dumped Steve for a boy at another school. Steve had never mentioned her in the two months that we'd been going together, but once when we were at a football game and watched her cheer, I said that I wished I was able to do it, too. Steve just squeezed my hand and said he liked me exactly the way I was.

Right then I wasn't even sure he remembered who I was. There was no doubt in my mind that he was enchanted. The question was whether he was caught up in the ski trip, with Heather, or both.

"I hate to do it," Heather said, and there was a genuine note of regret in her voice. "But I've really got to get going. The girls are waiting for me." She flashed him her famous smile. "Call me, and I'll give you more details about the trip. Should I give you my number, or do you still remember it?"

Steve laughed. "Five-five-five-nine-eight-seven-six."

"Right, exactly." Heather got up to leave, and over her shoulder she called, "Steve, I'm really glad you decided to come on the trip. We're going to have the most fantastic time."

Steve called back, "I'll bet we are!" Then he smiled at me.

I hoped that I didn't look as miserable as I felt. I hated feeling jealous, but I couldn't help it. His arm slid back around my shoulders, and he suddenly looked contrite. "Hey, babe, I'm sorry. I didn't mean to rub it in that I'm going and you're not. I guess I've been a real jerk; it's just that I'm so excited. You know how much I love to ski, and I haven't gotten to go since last winter."

I knew Steve was right, so I waited in silence as he finished his hot chocolate. He paid the check and helped me into my new coat. Suddenly I was very glad I'd chosen it in red. Red is really my best color, and I had a feeling I was going to need every advantage to keep Steve. We started to walk toward the door. "Darn, I should have asked Heather whether I should give the deposit to the ski club sponsor or take it to the school bookstore," he said. "Michelle, would you mind if I just ran back to Heather's table and asked her?"

I shook my head no, afraid that I wouldn't get the word out, and watched him head back to Heather. It was not one of the better moments of my life—me standing at the door all by myself and Steve halfway across the restaurant, engaged in laughing conversation with Heather. For one horrible moment I had the feeling that he was going to sit down and just leave me standing there.

After what seemed an eternity, Steve returned. We left the restaurant and walked silently, hand in hand, through the falling snow. There were just enough people on the sidewalk to turn the snow into a slushy mess. Cars zipped by, their noise coupling with the other sounds of the city to create a steady, familiar hum. I could only imagine how different the snowy scene at Vail would be. My vision of Vail was of a world of white, lighted by a big moon and lots of twinkling stars. The only interruptions would be the sounds of distant laughter and maybe a guitar being played in front of a cozy fire in the ski lodge.

I sighed softly. Steve seemed to pick up on it. "I'm going to miss you, too. But it's only ten days, and I'll be back for New Year's Eve. You'll see, it'll pass in a hurry. If you get that job at Klausner's Department Store, you'll probably be so busy that you won't even miss me."

I held his hand more tightly. "I'll miss you."

"Hey!" Steve said, changing the subject. "*Have* you heard anything about the job? Aren't they supposed to let you know soon?"

"I hope so. It's getting kind of late. But there isn't much I can do if they don't call."

"Well, I'll keep my fingers crossed for you. I just bet it comes through. I have a feeling we're both going to have good luck—me with getting to go on the ski trip and you with getting your first job."

I didn't say anything. "Well," Steve said, "maybe I should get you home, it's getting kind of late."

We drove home in silence, which was rare for us. We usually had so much to say. I knew that Steve was bursting to tell me more about the ski trip and that he was just waiting for the least bit of encouragement from me. But I couldn't do it, not that night. Maybe if we hadn't run into Heather, it wouldn't have been so bad. But after seeing them together in the coffee shop, it was clear that Steve was going to be well taken care of while we were apart. I just couldn't bear to listen to him talk about a trip that might take him away from me for good.

Pulling up in front of my house, Steve shut off the motor and turned toward me. His lips tenderly met mine. I wished his kiss could have lasted forever, but before I knew it, only its memory lingered on my lips, and I was sitting in my bedroom reflecting on the events of the evening. I wondered what effect they would have on my future.

Chapter Two

On Saturday morning I awoke to the sound of the telephone ringing. Usually I answered it by the first or second ring, but that morning I was too groggy to get it at all. The next thing I knew, Mom was standing in the doorway. "Michelle, quick, wake up! Mr. Johnson from personnel at Klausner's Department Store is on the phone for you."

I rubbed my eyes and cleared my throat, trying to wake myself in a hurry. My mouth felt all cottony, and nervousness gripped my stomach. I guessed I wanted the job more than I had realized.

"Mr. Johnson," I said, picking up the phone. I hoped my voice didn't reveal my nervousness. "This is Michelle."

"Michelle, I've got some good news for you. I think we'll be able to use you. I'm sorry it's so last minute, but I'd like you to come in this afternoon. You see, we're running a temporary employee training session that you really must attend."

I practically dropped the telephone, I was so surprised. But I tried to sound calm. I assured Mr. Johnson that I'd be there and wrote down the exact time and location of the training session. When I hung up, I noticed that Mom was hovering nearby. "Well—" she asked.

"I got the job!" I said in a daze.

Mom hugged me. "You're getting so grown-up. I just knew they'd realize how right you are for the job!"

I smiled to myself. One minute my mom was telling me how grown-up I was, and the next minute she was refusing me permission to do something because I was too young. My friends had the same problem with their parents, and we just sort of decided that parents couldn't make up their minds how to treat sixteen-year-olds.

Mom continued excitedly, "Tell me all about it, honey. When do you start? What kind of schedule will you have? Do you know what department you'll be working in?"

I could feel myself blushing. "Oh, Mom," I said, thinking maybe I wasn't so grown-up after all. "I forgot to ask any of those things. I was so nervous that I'd say the wrong thing and Mr. Johnson would change his mind. I just wanted to get off the phone."

Mom laughed. "It doesn't matter. You'll find out all the details soon enough. And don't worry about being nervous. Everyone's nervous in the beginning. I still remember my first job. I was eighteen, and I had gotten a summer job at the dime store. My first customers were an old man and a little boy. The child wanted a helium balloon. He spent ten minutes picking out just which balloon he wanted, and then I put it on the machine that inflated it with helium. The balloon got stuck and popped, and the little boy cried and cried. I wished I'd never gotten the job. But by a week later, I'd learned my way around the store and thought the job was lots of fun. I couldn't believe that I'd ever been scared."

I reached over and gave Mom a quick hug. She knew how frightened I was, and her story had been told to make me feel better. She helped me pick out a gray plaid skirt, a white button-down shirt, and a black blazer to wear to the training session. By the time I was dressed and ready to go, I felt pretty adult-looking.

I tried to call Steve to share the news with him, but there was no answer at his house. I felt a surge of disappointment, knowing he'd have been really excited for me. He'd been right when he'd said he had a feeling that we'd both get good news that weekend. Of course, my job couldn't affect my feelings for Steve. I wondered if he could say the same thing about his ski trip. I felt my eyes start to burn with the threat of tears and told myself that, at least for that afternoon, I'd have to put the whole thing out of my mind. If I didn't, I'd never be able to concentrate on my job training.

Mom offered to run me downtown to Klausner's, but I took the bus instead. Somehow, it just didn't seem nearly so grown-up to have Mom drop me off at work. The bus stop was only a couple of blocks from our house, and as I approached it, I could see a bus pulling away from the curb. That meant I had about a fifteen-minute wait before another one would come by.

The day was crisply cold, and there was only a little snow left. I loved the way the seasons changed in Denver; in Tucson you had to check a calendar to know what time of year it was. The bus finally arrived, and I pulled off my lined wool gloves to plunk my coins into the fare box. As the bus took its familiar route downtown, I thought about how many times I'd ridden it to go shopping. But now I'd be a store employee instead of a customer.

When I'd first suggested to my parents that I could get a part-time job, I was sure they'd say no. We'd been sitting at the dinner table, and Mom had been telling Dad how much trouble she'd had returning a tie she'd bought for him. "There just aren't enough salespeople in the stores. You have to wait forever to get help."

Dad thought that maybe it was hard for the stores to keep bright, honest young people in retail sales. They would want to move up or out. That started me thinking. Why couldn't I get a job in a department store? It would give me extra money for clothes and college, and it would prove to Mom and Dad that I was adult enough to take on the responsibility of a job.

I didn't really think Mom and Dad would go for the idea, but much to my surprise, they were very encouraging. Mom said, "I think you'd really enjoy it, but I only want you working during school vacations."

My father, who frequently complained about how flighty I was, put down his fork and smiled at me with new respect. I decided to start looking for a job immediately so that I could work over Christmas vacation. Mom suggested that I think about it for a few days, and if I was really serious, she'd take me downtown to get some applications for various stores.

When I remained determined to try to get a sales job, Mom and I started making the rounds. And while it had been a little scary to fill out the applications and go for the interviews, I felt a real sense of accomplishment afterward.

For a few days I crossed my fingers and checked every day after school with the stores. Then just as I'd gotten discouraged, someone in personnel at Klausner's Department Store had called me to say they were interested in hiring me and they'd let me know for sure in the next few weeks.

The bus snaked its way into the crowded downtown area, and I had to watch carefully so I'd know when to get off. Shoppers with packages were bustling everywhere. The bus arrived at my stop, and I pulled the wire.

Standing on the corner waiting for the traffic light to change, I had the crazy urge to turn to the people next to me and tell them that I wasn't just another shopper, I was an employee of Klausner's Department Store. But, of course, I didn't say anything to anyone.

In no time at all, I had reached Klausner's. I had to walk through the cosmetics department and go down the escalator in order to reach the employee training room. When I entered the room, I saw that there were about ten other people already there. I noticed two cash registers on nearby tables.

I sat in a chair, wondering what the training session would be like. Soon a no-nonsense-looking woman with a gold badge strode into the room. Her badge said: Klausner's Training Supervisor—Mrs. Higgins.

"I'd like to welcome you all to Klausner's. I've worked for this store for seventeen years, and I can tell you that it is an excellent firm. You're what we call temps, that's short for temporary help, and you will be moved throughout the store as we need you. In most cases your employment will be for a short period of time, and your hours may vary from day to day. The Christmas season is, without a doubt, the most hectic time of the year. Though your training will be short, it is important that you understand fully every procedure we cover. Our other employees will not have time to help you, and mistakes can be costly for all of us."

With that she launched into an explanation of a cash register, demonstrating on one that was nearby. She also explained the store's code numbers and how to ring up a cash versus a credit card sale and which credit cards were accepted by the store. There was a number we had to call for authorization before accepting credit purchases over a certain amount. Just as I took a deep breath, Mrs. Higgins pushed her glasses up on the bridge of her nose and said, "Unless you have any questions, we'll proceed to exchanges."

I never realized that there could be so much to exchanging an item. I thought about the blue shirt that I'd decided to exchange for one in red. It had seemed simple enough to me, and I couldn't understand what had taken the salesgirl so long to complete the exchange. Now I was much more sympathetic.

Finally Mrs. Higgins announced that we'd take a short break before she covered merchandise returns. I was afraid that by the time I got another set of instructions, I'd have forgotten what I'd learned about ringing up a simple cash sale. After getting a drink of water, I glanced at the faces of the rest of the trainees. Most everyone looked a little bewildered, and it felt good to know I wasn't the only one.

Our break ended quickly, and Mrs. Higgins pushed up the sleeves of her beige sweater and started explaining returns. My head was spinning with numbers by the time she stopped. "Now, if you'll just line up behind one of the two registers, we're going to give you each a chance to practice the things you've learned. You'll be asked to ring up a sale, a cash return, a merchandise credit, and an exchange. At each register you'll find a list of situations in which a customer comes to you with a transaction. Ring up the first 'sale' and bring me the sales slip so I can check to see that you've done it correctly. After I've OK'ed the slip, you can get in line to perform the next transaction."

Waiting for my turn, I had the same kind of butterflies in my stomach that I usually got during chemistry tests. I didn't know what I'd expected, but I sure hadn't thought I'd have to take a *test* to get to be a salesperson.

I got through the cash sale and exchange just fine, and I was feeling pretty confident. The next situation on the list said, "A teenager brings in a skirt to return. She doesn't want any other merchandise, and she says that since she was given the skirt as a gift, she doesn't have a receipt. You check and find out the skirt cost twenty-four dollars."

It seemed simple enough. I entered the proper

codes and ticket price, but when I pressed the last button, the machine just stopped. No return slip, nothing. Mrs. Higgins had to come over, and it took her a few minutes to figure out how the cash register had jammed and how to clear it again.

She said she wasn't sure if I had made a mistake or not, but she made me practice three returns anyway, to make certain I'd gotten it right. I was shaking by the time I finally sat down, but I was also pretty sure that I'd never make a mistake again on a return.

I figured we must be about finished. What else could they have to teach us? But Mrs. Higgins informed us that we'd be taking another ten-minute break, and then a buyer and a person from store security would speak with us.

When we regrouped ten minutes later, a short lady with flaming red hair and a tall, broad-shouldered man joined us. Much to my surprise, the woman turned out to be the representative from store security. She spoke to us about the increased shoplifting problems that occurred during Christmas, told us what to do if we saw someone shoplifting, and sternly warned us that all store employees were expected to watch for shoplifters, and more importantly, prevent merchandise from being stolen. She spoke to us firmly and with great emphasis. I was reminded of my English teacher, who seemed to put exclamation points after each of her sentences.

The tall man who looked like a football player turned out to be one of the buyers for the store. He talked to us about how important it was to keep the sales area neat and the dressing rooms cleared of merchandise.

Finally Mrs. Higgins stood up and removed her glasses. "If there are no questions, that will end your training. Stop by personnel on your way out to get your schedule and name badge. Congratulations, and again, welcome to Klausner's!"

Chapter Three

"Hi, I'm Jane," said a dark-haired lady in the personnel department. "You'll check with me for your schedule and please let me know if you run into any problems." I nodded. "Now let's see. Your application says you can work full-time between December twenty-first and December thirty-first and part-time for a few days before and after those dates. Is that still correct?"

I nodded yes again. Jane glanced at the calendar on her desk. "OK, today's December twelfth." She called up some information on the computer and then continued. "I'll definitely need you next Friday from five to nine and for the moonlight sale on Saturday, the nineteenth. Then you'll work pretty much full-time from Monday the twenty-first through New Year's."

I gulped. Saturday night was the last night that Steve was going to be home; I wanted to

21

spend it with him. "Uh, Saturday night could be kind of a problem."

Jane's smile faded immediately. "Oh, dear, we really are going to need lots of extra help that night; the Saturday before Christmas is usually our busiest day, and the sale will only add to that. I'd really like to have you come in from eleven to three and then again in the evening from five until nine."

Deciding that I'd better not say no or I might lose my job before I even got started, I reluctantly agreed to work on Saturday. At least I'd get off early enough to see Steve after work.

"Excellent," she said. "Then I'll see you on Friday the eighteenth and Saturday the nineteenth. Check with me after you punch in to find out where to report. Here's your employee identification tag." Jane handed me a square badge encased in plastic that had Klausner's printed in script across the top and Ms. Gunderson neatly typed below it.

I stared at the badge. I was no longer just a girl named Michelle. I was now Ms. Gunderson. My heart was pounding with excitement, and I knew just who I wanted to share my news with.

Finding the pay phones, I dropped in a quarter and dialed. Maybe Steve could pick me up and be the first to see "Ms. Gunderson" after her initiation into the working world. The phone rang, and Steve's mother answered it. "Oh, Michelle, he's been gone since early this morning. He went shopping for some things for his ski trip, and then he said he was going to a late-afternoon meeting at Heather's house. Shall I tell him to call you when he comes home?"

"No, that's all right," I replied. "In fact, you don't even need to tell him I called since I'm going to see him later tonight anyway."

I hung up the receiver, put my name badge in my purse, and began to walk to the bus stop. Somehow the thrill of getting my job didn't last long knowing that Steve was with Heather. I wondered if anyone else had been at their "meeting." After all, Heather had been Steve's girlfriend, and she had been the one to dump him. She was one of the cutest girls in school, and she obviously wanted Steve back. How could I compete with her when the two of them were just about to spend ten days together skiing in one of the most romantic spots in the world? I hated feeling jealous and wasn't normally a jealous person, but this wasn't a normal situation, either.

A bus finally arrived, and I rode home in silence, consumed by thoughts of Steve and Heather. As I reached my stop, I noticed the wind had begun to blow, and I pulled on my gloves and pushed my unruly hair under a red knit hat.

As soon as I got home, my mom asked me how everything had gone. I told her about the whole afternoon in detail and how my first evening at work would be the following Friday. Then, trying to keep my voice casual, I asked her if anyone had called while I'd been gone.

She laughed. "No calls, honey. You may feel as if you've been gone for a long time, but you were only out for the afternoon."

She went into the kitchen to check on dinner, and I hung up my blazer. Steve had mentioned that he thought we'd see a movie that night, but we really hadn't decided which movie or what time. Maybe he was so busy at Heather's that he'd forgotten all about our date, I thought miserably.

As if on cue the phone rang, and I rushed to grab it. "Steve!" I exclaimed with happy relief when I heard his voice. But before I could say much more, he said that he really couldn't talk then. He promised to come over to pick me up at eight. I heard someone giggling in the background and other voices. It sounded like a party. Steve rushed to say goodbye.

After I hung up, I realized I hadn't even had a chance to tell him about my job or my training. And he hadn't mentioned a word about going to Heather's for a meeting, though it was obvious that he wasn't calling from home.

I walked into the kitchen, but I wasn't really hungry. In fact, between the nervousness I'd felt all day at the training seminar and the hollow feeling in my stomach because of Steve, I felt absolutely exhausted. Dad was sitting at the kitchen table and greeted me by saying, "Hello,

Ms. Gunderson," and asking to see the famous name badge.

My ten-year-old brother, Scott, couldn't stand my getting all the attention, so between mouthfuls of french fries he said, "So did you make a bunch of mistakes today?"

My dad looked at Scott sternly and then encouraged me to tell him about my afternoon. I described it to him even though I didn't much feel like it. I knew there was no point in telling him I was depressed about Steve because he thought we saw too much of each other already.

After I finished dinner and helped my mom with the dishes, I went to my room to get dressed for my date. Turning on the light, I thought again how lucky I was to have such a perfect bedroom. My mom had let me choose the wallpaper, which was white with little blue and lavender hearts on it. Then we found some lavender satin heart pillows to go with it. When I remembered to make my bed, they looked terrific against my navy comforter.

I sat down on the bed, hugging one of the pillows. Steve's phone call had upset me, and I had to figure out whether to talk to him about it or ignore it. I finally decided to subtly work the call into the evening's conversation. Maybe then I'd find out why he'd been in such a hurry to get off the phone.

I pulled out a pair of jeans as well as a pair of blue wool slacks. Trying to decide if I wanted to look sporty or sophisticated, I wondered briefly which Heather would choose. Not that it mattered, but it seemed to me that she rarely wore jeans. Staring at both pairs of pants again, I impulsively stuffed the jeans back in the closet. The blue wool slacks with a fuzzy, yellow turtleneck sweater and chunky blue beads created a pretty outfit. I felt quite sophisticated. Running a comb through my hair, I squinted into the mirror and wondered what I'd look like with long, blond hair. But even with my eyes half-closed and my imagination at its best, I couldn't picture it. I sighed. Either you had that cheerleader look or you didn't, and I didn't.

Just as I dabbed on perfume and finished applying lipstick, the door bell rang. When I got to the living room, Scott was there babbling to Steve. A few weeks ago I'd overheard Scott tell Steve that he wanted to grow up to be just like him, except he didn't want to waste time on any girlfriends. Heaven only knew what else he'd been telling Steve.

Steve was wearing a dark brown ski sweater. Seeing me, he looked up and smiled. Those incredibly blue eyes melted my heart. "Well, Scott says you've had quite an afternoon."

I gave Scott a dirty look. Telling Steve about my job was something I'd wanted to do. Scott stared back. "I didn't tell him what it was, honest. I just said you had something real special to tell him, and that I already knew all about it."

"True," Steve said in a melodramatic tone. "Even though I threatened to torture him, he never told me his sister's great secret!"

I laughed, and so did Scott. Then I asked Steve if he wanted to look at the paper so we could decide on a movie. He blushed, which was highly unlike Steve. "Uh, a bunch of kids are going roller-skating tonight, and I kind of told them we'd meet them. Of course, we don't have to if you don't want to," he added quickly.

My heart skipped a beat. A voice inside me said, *A bunch of kids, huh. Why doesn't he just say Heather and her friends? Who does he think he's kidding?*

For heaven's sake, argued another voice, *quit being so paranoid.*

But the first voice wouldn't give up. *Didn't he just spend the whole afternoon at Heather's? Didn't his own mother say he was there? Why don't you just ask him who else is going tonight?*

"Hey, Michelle, you in there?" Steve asked. "You look as if you're somewhere in outer space. Listen, if you don't want to go skating, we won't go."

I kept my voice deliberately casual. "Oh, it's OK. Who else is going?"

Steve explained that Heather had told him practically everyone who was going on the ski trip would be at the skating rink that night to get their leg muscles in shape. "I'd really like to go," he said. "Most of the kids have been toning up for a while, but since I joined very late, I don't have much time to get in shape."

I forced a smile. "I'll just go change into some jeans. Scott, why don't you keep Steve company?" Scott seemed thrilled about the extra time with Steve, and Steve seemed delighted that I'd agreed to go skating. But I wasn't happy about anything, and I began to feel like Scrooge. "Bah, humbug" on everyone's excitement.

While I pulled on my jeans, I began arguing with myself again. I told myself that Steve was embarrassed and reluctant to tell me about everything connected with the ski trip because he felt bad that he was going without me. My other self said that the real reason he seemed embarrassed was that it wasn't easy to be around two girlfriends at the same time, especially when he was no longer certain which one was in the past and which one was in the present.

I took a deep breath, got my coat, and went to rejoin Steve. As soon as we were out of the house, he took my hand and asked what my secret was.

"I got the job at Klausner's."

He let out a loud whoop and gave me a big hug. Opening the car door for me, he said he wanted to know every detail. I had really only intended to give him a brief summary of the day, but he seemed so interested and asked so many questions, that I just kept talking. In no time we were pulling up to the skating rink halfway across town.

As we got out of the car, I wished I'd asked more about the evening. I had no idea who or how many people were going to be there or how well they skated. My questions didn't go unanswered for long, however. The rink was fairly empty, and it was easy to spot a group of about fifteen kids from Washington. In all, I'd been told fifty kids were going on the ski trip, and I wondered where the rest of them were.

Heather beckoned us over, and while Steve went to get our skates, I asked her where the rest of the ski group was that night. She looked at me with arched eyebrows. "I think everyone who matters is here."

Before I could think of a reply, Steve came back with our skates. As we laced them, we watched Heather skate. From what I gathered, she wasn't with a date. Heather looked totally at ease skating both forward and backward, and she was clearly the best one on the floor. I, on the other hand, could barely skate. Every kid eventually learns how, and even I had finally caught on. That didn't mean any fancy stuff; it just meant I could get around the rink without killing myself.

To my surprise it was fun skating hand in hand with Steve. By the time they'd played a couple of songs, I had almost forgotten about

Heather. But keeping up with Steve was no easy task, and after about seven songs, I knew I had to rest. "Steve," I gasped, "what do you say we sit a few out."

"Come on, let's skate a couple more first."

"I've got a good idea. *You* skate a couple more. I'll watch while I rest." I skated off the rink and sat down. My legs seemed to continue to roll along, but my body was gratefully immobile. I leaned my head back against the chair and closed my eyes. What a day it had been. I'd gotten my first job, gone through an afternoon of training, and was now out roller-skating. No wonder I was exhausted!

I'm not sure how long I dozed, but the last thing I remembered hearing was the steady rhythm of a fast rock tune. Now the soft sounds of a ballad were playing. The rink was bathed in darkness except for the twinkling made by a mirrored ball suspended from the middle of the ceiling. Everyone on the floor was skating in couples. There were a lot of kids milling around the sidelines, and two girls plunked themselves down on the bench, which was next to my chair. I couldn't help but overhear them remark that they hated it whenever the announcer called "couples only skate" because there never seemed to be a cute boy nearby who'd ask them to skate.

I looked around for Steve, wondering where he'd gone and wishing we were skating together like the shadowy figures that passed by. The two girls next to me continued talking. "Ooh," one of the girls said. "Look at that couple over there on the other side of the rink. They're really good! I bet they come here all the time." My eyes followed her finger. The pair was skating as if they were one. Transfixed, I watched them as they skated closer to my side of the rink. Their faces whizzed by in a semiblur, but it wasn't so dark that I couldn't recognize the magical couple as Steve and Heather.

The song ended, and the announcer called, "Everyone skate!" The lights were turned back up, and the beat of a rock song once again filled the air. Heather and Steve stood on the rink floor indecisively, and then Steve looked over at me. He said something to Heather, and the two of them skated off the floor to the rest area where I was sitting.

Heather was still holding his arm when they reached me, and her green, catlike eyes flashed triumphantly. "Well," she drawled, "nap time all finished?" Not waiting for my answer, she turned toward Steve. "That was lots of fun. You're a terrific skater."

"Nah," Steve replied, but his eyes were sparkling. "Really you're the one who does all the fancy stuff out there."

I wondered if they were going to stand there complimenting each other all night long. Heather pulled at the purple ribbon around her golden ponytail. "I can hardly wait to see us on

31

the ski slopes. Just think, next week at this time we'll be packing."

Steve said he could hardly wait either. Heather looked as though she had more to say, but then someone called her back on the floor. Steve and I stood looking awkwardly at each other as she departed. I was too furious to say anything at all.

Finally Steve said, "You must have been really tired. You slept for about half an hour. I thought about waking you but—"

I finished the sentence for him, "You found Heather instead."

Steve's jaw tightened. Through gritted teeth he said, "You know, I think we should just call it a night. I'll take you home."

Chapter Four

Usually I sat close to Steve in the car, but right then I wasn't sure where I wanted to sit. After all, I was the one who should be mad, not Steve. But instead of apologizing for skating with Heather, he was ending the evening. I moved nearer to the passenger side and waited for some kind of explanation. It seemed none was coming.

We drove on in silence, and the tension grew. I could hardly believe that it had been only a week before that we'd discussed how positively, absolutely right we were for each other.

My mind wandered back to the previous Saturday night. We'd decided we felt like doing something really silly. So, in the middle of a snowstorm, we'd taken our bathing suits and gone swimming. There was a place in Denver that had two enclosed tube slides that wrapped around the building and splashed into an indoor, Olympic-sized swimming pool. As we got out of the pool, I'd told Steve what a wonderful time I'd had. He'd put his arm around me and whispered that all our times together were pretty terrific.

How could things have changed so much in so little time? This evening it looked as if he would have preferred to be with Heather. Whatever he felt, I just wished he'd tell me what was going on. But in my heart, I was afraid I already knew. After all, my mother had always told me that actions spoke louder than words.

Still, I just kept hoping for some kind of an explanation about Heather. Why couldn't Steve just say that he was sorry if he'd been insensitive to my feelings? Why couldn't he tell me that she was an impossible flirt but that she didn't mean anything at all to him?

We got to my house, and Steve switched off the motor. His voice sounded strained as he said, "Come on, I'll walk you to your door." I couldn't stand for the evening to end this way, and in spite of myself, I could feel the tears welling up in my eyes.

Steve looked over at me. "I guess it wasn't the best time we've ever had. I-I'm sorry. Maybe we should have skipped going skating."

Bolstered by his apology, I decided that everything would be fine if we could discuss Heather, if I could just know that she wasn't a threat. "Steve," I began, "about Heather—"

There was an edge to his voice as he cut me off.

"For pete's sake, Michelle, all I did was skate with her. Why are you making it into such a big deal?"

I wanted to ask him why he was being so defensive about the whole thing if it was no big deal, but I had a feeling that my questions would only make things worse. Maybe we needed to wait until another night when neither of us was feeling edgy. I asked Steve when we'd see each other before he left. By the time we went through our schedules, we realized it wasn't going to be easy to see each other at all. We both had exams coming up in almost every subject. Steve's mother had made him promise to spend a couple of nights visiting the relatives he'd normally have seen on Christmas. And then, of course, there were the last-minute ski club meetings he just *had* to attend. "By the time I signed up for this trip, most of the work had been done. The least I can do is show up at the last couple of meetings."

We went through our whole schedules and realized that we could only see each other Saturday night after I got off work. I sensed that Steve was sort of relieved that we wouldn't have more time together.

He walked me to the door and gave me a quick kiss on the cheek. "Michelle, I'm really glad you got your job. But I think we're both pretty tired, so I'll say good night."

I wanted to say something to keep the evening

from ending that way, but I wasn't sure what. I didn't want to do anything that would make things worse instead of better. So I went in the house and stood in front of the large living room window, pulling the drape back enough to watch Steve walk to his car. As the blue Trans Am pulled away from the curb, I wondered if I'd ever see it there in the future. Maybe Steve was right. We were probably both so tired that we were overreacting. On the other hand, maybe Steve was confused and fishing for time to decide which girlfriend he really liked.

I was still standing in the living room when my mom came in. "Well, it's only eleven. I didn't expect you home yet. How was roller-skating?"

I told her that it hadn't been too terrific and that I would tell her about it another time. One thing I really loved about my Mom was that she never pushed me when I didn't feel like talking.

After I had gotten ready for bed, I sat in my room thinking that maybe I should tell my mom about my problems with Steve after all. She might have some advice about the whole thing. I really didn't have any one girlfriend that I knew well enough to discuss Steve with. I had made lots of friends since I'd been in Denver, but they weren't the kind of I-can-tell-you-anything friends I had had back in Tucson. I climbed into bed and decided that I'd wait a few days before I said anything. Maybe things would just work themselves out. I turned out the lights and mentally crossed my fingers. Life would be very bleak without Steve.

I fell asleep and dreamed about the party Steve had given me the month before. We'd gone over to his house, supposedly to watch TV. But when we got there, a bunch of kids jumped out of hiding places and yelled "Surprise." The whole living room had been decorated for a birthday party. Perplexed, I'd looked at Steve. It wasn't my birthday. He'd explained that since I'd turned sixteen shortly before I'd come to Colorado, he thought I should get a new party with my new friends—an "unbirthday" party. That night we'd danced and laughed, and Steve had never left my side. But now, in my dreams, everything was twisted. The party was exactly the same, but suddenly a clock chimed ten, and Steve said, "Well, goodbye, Michelle. Heather, this is now your party." Everyone cheered, and Heather, wearing a white ski outfit, took Steve's hand. The party then continued as if I'd never been there at all. I woke up shaking my head in bewilderment. I told myself it was only a stupid dream, but Monday at school, I suddenly felt shy when Steve slid into his seat in front of me in history.

The week was so crazily hectic that Steve and I barely even got a chance to talk on the phone, let alone see each other. On Friday in history he passed me a note that wished me good luck at my first night of work and said he was going to a family dinner at his Aunt Emily's. He promised to call me if he got home early enough.

I'd been hoping that he'd be able to pick me up after work and hear all about my first night, but if he couldn't, at least I'd know it wasn't because he was with Heather.

The bell rang at three o'clock, and a cheer rose up throughout the school. By the time I got home I was very nervous. I grabbed a granola bar and pulled out the employee manual I'd been given at the training seminar. I read it, then reread it.

Mom volunteered to take me to work and pick me up that first night. At four she came into the kitchen to tell me that she thought I'd better get ready. I'd already planned exactly what I was going to wear. I pulled out my navy blue wool skirt and white crewneck sweater. Dressing quickly, I added a blue-and-green-patterned scarf around my neck. I slipped into a pair of navy flats, hoping my feet wouldn't kill me after standing on them for four straight hours. After brushing my hair and putting on some lipstick, I was ready for the final touch. I stood in front of the mirror as I carefully pinned "Ms. Gunderson" on my sweater.

Scott wandered in. "Hey, you don't look too bad." I smiled. From Scott that was really a compliment. Then it was time to leave. Mom tried to make small talk on the way downtown, but I was too nervous to pay attention to what she was saying. First it seemed to take forever to get there, and then suddenly we were in front of the store.

"I guess I'd better get out," I said, suddenly wishing we were going back home.

"You'll do just fine. I know you will," Mom said as I got out of the car. Before she pulled away, she called out to remind me that she'd pick me up at this spot at nine-fifteen.

Well, Michelle, I thought. *This is it. You wanted this job, you've got it. Now the question is, can you do it?*

I walked inside and headed for the personnel department. Jane was behind the counter. "Hi, Ms. Gunderson." I smiled, feeling pleased that she'd remembered me; then I realized I had taken off my coat and that she had been reading my name tag. "Why don't you put your coat in an employee locker and punch in over there." As I did so, she began punching keys on the computer. "Now, let's see. I've scheduled you to work in ski accessories tonight. Do you know where that department is located?"

When I shook my head, she circled a place on a store map and handed it to me. Then she turned her attention to someone who'd come in after me. I felt rooted to the spot. "Excuse me," Jane said to the person. "Uh, Ms. Gunderson. You can go ahead and report to the ski department."

I took the escalator back up to the main floor and walked to the department. There was a tall, balding man at the register ringing up a ski hat. I waited until he was finished and then introduced myself. He looked at me appraisingly. "You a temporary?"

I nodded my head.

"How long you been working?"

I swallowed hard. "Uh, tonight's my first night." The man groaned and then went off to help a lady who wanted some ski gloves.

As I watched him go, a voice said, "Excuse me, miss, do you work in this department?"

I turned to see a grandmotherly lady with two Ski Colorado pins. I took them from her and started to ring them up, hoping that I'd punched in all the numbers correctly. When the register spit out a correct completed sales slip, I felt ecstatic. The lady paid; I gave her her change, and she departed with her package.

I'd done it, and it hadn't even been that hard! Of course, not every sale was that smooth. At one point I'd been interrupted by a man who wanted information on ski wax. I was in the middle of ringing up some gloves, and I mistakenly punched the keys for a charge instead of cash sale. I had had to void the register and start again. But, all in all, things were going pretty well. I glanced at my watch, and to my surprise, I only had another half hour before the store closed. It was really sort of fun.

"Well, I didn't know you were working here." I turned to see Heather Lance, her golden curls perfectly arranged, staring over the counter at me. Her green eyes flashed as she sweetly said, "Actually, I'm glad you're here. You see, I need to get a special Christmas present. Maybe you could help me pick it out."

She flashed that angelic smile and waited for my response. The last thing in the world I wanted to do was help Heather Lance with anything. I stammered that I'd been so busy that I really hadn't had time to familiarize myself with the merchandise. That wasn't entirely true. In fact, as soon as I'd noticed the pale blue ski hats, I knew one of them would be my Christmas gift to Steve. There were only four left, and I'd already put one behind the counter to be rung up later on my employee discount card. Not only would the color be perfect with Steve's blue eyes, but also he'd mentioned that he really wanted another ski hat.

I advised Heather that she might want to look at the Ski Colorado pins and went gratefully to another customer. The woman was asking whether I thought her nephew would rather have gloves or mittens. The customer decided on gloves, but then she couldn't choose between black and gray. Finally I helped her select a pair of gray mittens. When I had finished ringing up her purchase, I noticed that not only was Heather still in the department, but also she was holding the same blue ski hat that I'd picked out for Steve. "Somehow, the pin didn't seem quite right. This hat, though, is special, don't you think?" she asked.

I bit my lip and said nothing, but Heather didn't really want my answer anyway. "I'll take it," she added. I tried to keep my hands from shaking as I rung up her hat and told her the amount. It was uncanny. How could we both have picked exactly the same item out of an entire department, unless, of course, that item was for the same person? With a sinking heart, I knew I was right. Heather and I had both realized how perfect that blue would be with Steve's eyes.

She took the package from me, saying it was really too bad that I couldn't go on the ski trip. Heather looked smugly confident as she left the department. I stared after her with such anger that I didn't even notice Mr. Holden come up behind me. "Well, it's time to wrap up another night. You didn't do half bad for a brand-new temp. Come on, I'll show you how to close out the register for the night."

I felt pretty proud of myself. One void wasn't too bad, and a couple of the customers had even remarked about how helpful I'd been. Mr. Holden reached under the counter for a close-out form, and with it he pulled out the blue ski hat I'd been planning to buy for Steve. "If you're saving this for a customer, you've got to put her name on it. If it was returned, get it out on the floor so we can resell it."

"It—it was for me," I said, thinking of Heather. "But I've changed my mind." I took the hat from him and put it back among the other ski hats, knowing it was just perfect for Steve. Of course, Heather had never actually said that the one she bought was for him. But then again, did she really have to?

Mr. Holden closed out the register, and the bell sounded. A voice came over the store loudspeaker. "Klausner's is now closed for the evening. We will open at ten tomorrow. Thank you for shopping with us."

The bustling store emptied out, and Mr. Holden turned to me. "Follow me. Employees have to leave this way." I went downstairs with him to punch out and get my coat. A guard was checking the employee packages. For a moment I stood looking at all those people laden with Christmas gifts and wondered how I'd ever find a present for Steve before he left. My gift had to be perfect, not only because I really liked Steve but also because I wanted him to think of me the whole time he was skiing with Heather.

Walking through the line of employees, I headed for the door hoping that Steve had finished his family dinner early and called my mom to say he'd pick me up. But when I got to the street, I saw my mother's old red station wagon waiting for me.

Chapter Five

When I checked in at work on Saturday morning, I didn't feel nearly so nervous as I had on Friday, especially after Jane told me that Mr. Holden had requested me back in his department. Jane laughed wryly, saying, "We featured two items from ski accessories in the newspaper ad we ran today, so I'm sure Jim Holden will welcome your appearance."

I headed toward ski accessories, making my way through the jam-packed aisles. People bustled everywhere, carrying bulky packages and bags. Huge wreaths, decorated with red ribbons and gold ornaments, hung from the store ceiling, adding to the festive mood.

There were customers lined up at the register when I arrived, and Mr. Holden looked ragged. "Can you believe this crowd? They put out all these gloves reduced from thirty to fifteen dollars, and people are falling all over one another to buy them." The atmosphere was amazing. I began trying to help three and four people at a time. Some of them looked as if they were having a great time, while others seemed to hate the whole Christmas season. Everyone called me Ms. Gunderson and looked at me as if I knew what I was doing. I began to feel both important and useful.

Before I knew it, it was three o'clock. I was off from three to five and rather than going home and coming back, I'd told my mom I'd just stay downtown and shop. Of course, that was before I'd been on my feet for four hours. Stopping in the employee cafeteria, I ordered myself a large chocolate shake and sank into a chair. Suddenly every bone in my body felt heavy and tired. My feet were throbbing, and I slipped them out of the black pumps I'd been wearing. I didn't see any way I could shop for the next two hours and then work for an additional four. Still, if I didn't get Steve his Christmas present that night, I wouldn't have a chance to give it to him before he left.

The milk shake was cold and deliciously sweet, but definitely not substantial enough to last me until I got off work. I resolved to get something else to eat and then continue looking for something for Steve. I'd just have to wait until the next day, when Steve would be gone and I'd be off work, to collapse. But when I stood up to leave, I couldn't get my shoes back on my feet. I'd been standing for so long, both the previous evening and that morning, that my toes were swollen and rebelling. Painfully, I shoved them back into the pumps and wondered how I could have ever thought those shoes were comfortable.

Grabbing a hot dog, I left the employee cafeteria and entered the madness. As busy as it was now, they were expecting a much larger crowd in the evening at the store's Merry Moonlight Christmas promotion. From five until closing, sale items in the store would be marked down an additional twenty percent.

With the strains of "Jingle Bells" playing in the background, I entered the men's department and hoped I'd see something that was just right for Steve. I looked at shirts first. There were some nice ones, but nothing extraordinary. I thought about going up to the record department and getting him a couple of tapes, but that didn't seem quite right either. I stood in the men's department, wondering whether it would be better to get Steve a shirt so I'd have something to give him or whether I should wait and try to find something extra special to give him when he got back. While I agonized, time slipped away, and the choice was taken out of my hands. I had to be back in my department to work.

"I don't think we're going to be that busy tonight," said Mr. Holden when I got back. "We've pretty much sold out of the gloves, and those were the biggest seller in our department. The ski goggles they featured in the ad are very nice, but they're cheaper at the sporting goods store down the street." Mr. Holden was right. The store was soon jammed with people, but our department was pretty well bypassed. I stood watching the stationery department across the aisle, where they were having a sale on wrapping paper and greeting cards. Hordes of last-minute shoppers grabbed and pushed to get the best of the remaining items.

"Amazing, isn't it," said Mr. Holden. "Do you think they have any idea what they're getting? They just want something before we run out."

Just then a short, elf of a man walked up to us. "You folks sure are lucky. It's empty over here. In men's sportswear they're standing three deep to the register." Mr. Holden introduced me to the speaker, who had been a good friend and coworker for years. "Listen, Jim," he said to Mr. Holden. "You won't believe what they dug out of the warehouse. We've got six of those Fila sweaters—you know, the ones that sold for a hundred dollars. Well, the orders with them said to mark them at twenty-nine ninety-nine and clear them out tonight. I'm buying one for my son, and I put one aside for you."

Mr. Holden whistled. "Sure is a steal, Bill, especially after our discount. Thanks." He turned to me. "Michelle, I'm taking my break. Please keep an eye on the department."

As the two men walked away, I yelled after them, "Wait! If they have one of those Fila sweaters that is blue and a large, will you put it aside for me?" Mr. Conrad gave me an OK sign and disappeared into the milling crowd. The music lilting through the store was all about peace on earth, but that night's scene looked anything but peaceful.

Before Mr. Holden finally returned, I sold several pairs of gloves, a hat, and two pairs of goggles. "Those sweaters are gorgeous," he crowed. "You'd better get over there immediately. Ask for Bill."

My heart was pounding as I arrived at men's sportswear. There was a line a mile long curling around the register. I didn't see how I'd ever get anyone to help me before I had to get back. Fortunately Mr. Conrad saw me and waved. I kept excusing myself as I made my way over to him, but I still got a lot of dirty looks. I knew the sweater was perfect for Steve the minute Mr. Conrad pulled it from behind the counter. It was midnight blue with a pale blue racing stripe down each sleeve. "I'll take it," I said.

Mr. Conrad talked as he filled out the employee discount forms. "Lucky for you that this sweater was left. There's only one other one, and it's an extra small. Going to take a boy to wear that."

Maybe it was because I'd found the ideal gift for Steve or maybe it was because there really was something called Christmas spirit and good will toward men. I don't know. But the last sweater was there on the sale table, and I knew the bright red would look great against Scott's dark hair. Suddenly I found myself saying I'd take that one, too. As Bill looked for a shopping bag, I thought smugly to myself, *Who says I never do anything nice for my brother?*

I thanked Mr. Conrad and started back. As I walked, I realized that I'd just spent more money than I'd earned for the day. It was a good thing that Dad had advanced me some money for "pre-paycheck" Christmas shopping.

It was too bad I wouldn't have time to wait in line to get Steve's sweater wrapped, but it didn't matter. I knew he'd love it anyway; I couldn't have found a more perfect present if I'd tried for the entire year. I could hardly wait for the store to close so I could give it to him.

When I got back to ski accessories, Mr. Holden shot me a desperate look. Several people were in line waiting to be helped. I knew that I wasn't entitled to a break at all, and I was sorry that I'd been gone so long.

At last nine o'clock arrived, and the wonderful words, "Thank you for shopping at Klausner's. The store is now closed," rang out over the loudspeakers. It took almost another twenty minutes for the store to empty of customers. The poor ladies in stationery were trying to put their department back into some order. Wrapping

49

paper, ribbons, and isolated cards were strewn everywhere. I straightened gloves and goggles while Mr. Holden wearily closed out the register.

"Well," I said as we walked toward the line for employees with packages, "thanks for everything and thanks again a million times for letting me get the ski sweaters. I sure hope I get to work with you in ski accessories again next week."

The lady in package checkout matched up my forms and told me to go ahead. Mr. Holden waved goodbye. Stepping out the door and into the swirling snow, I strained to see Steve's blue Trans Am. It was nowhere to be found. With a sinking feeling, I clutched my package of ski sweaters and hoped he hadn't forgotten.

Just as I was trying to decide whether I should go back into the store and call, he pulled up. Leaning over, he opened the door on the passenger side of the car. "Your chariot, or tonight, better make that your sleigh, awaits you."

I climbed in, shook the snow from my hair, and smiled at him. No matter how much time Steve and I spent together, each time I saw him he looked even handsomer. Never had I been as crazy about a guy as I was about Steve. I was happy just to be sitting next to him, warm from the car heater, watching the snow fall.

Steve started to tell me about his day. He said he'd never been as excited about anything in his life as he was about the ski trip. That was why he'd been late. He'd been at Heather's for a while, and then he'd been busy checking up on some last-minute details. I was torn between feeling excited for him and sorry for me because he hadn't mentioned thinking about me at all.

"So," he said, "what will it be? You want to go to your house, my house, out for hot chocolate? You call it." I decided we should go back to my house because I didn't want to give him the ski sweater in some restaurant. I wanted the moment to be romantic and memorable.

As we walked to the door, he finally noticed the bulky package in my hand. "Wow, did you work today, or did you just buy the place out?" he asked, and then offered to carry the bag. "What's in here anyway?"

"That's for me to know and you to find out— maybe," I said. I tried to push aside the small twinge of hurt I felt because he was carrying no package for me.

Mom and Dad were in the family room watching TV, and I stopped in to tell them about my day. Dad kidded Steve that if it kept snowing, he could ski right here in Denver. Steve laughed, and then he and I went into the living room. There was still a big fire blazing in the fireplace, and we sat on the floor in front of it, leaning back against the sofa.

Watching the flames dance in the fireplace and the snow swirl outside the window was mesmerizing. Neither of us said a word. Steve had his arm around me, and I felt as if I were in heaven. I thought I might burst with happiness.

After a while my parents stopped in to say good night on their way upstairs. I began feeling sleepy myself. The day had been so hectic that I just wanted to rest, but I knew I had to make the night last. Steve turned to face me and whispered, "I'm going to miss you, you know."

I could feel the tears welling up in my eyes. I didn't want him to see me cry, so I jumped up, saying, "I have your Christmas present. I'm sorry I didn't get it wrapped." Suddenly I felt a little shy about giving it to him. I fished in the bag, pulling the price tag off. "Now close your eyes and put out your hands." He did, and as I bent to place the sweater in his arms, I couldn't help but notice his long, thick eyelashes. "OK, open your eyes."

He stared at the sweater for a second, then his mouth dropped open. "Oh, Michelle, it's beautiful. I'll be the best-dressed guy on the slopes. The pale blue stripe on the sleeve even matches my new hat." He blushed, and I couldn't help but wonder if it was because the hat made him think of Heather.

I made up my mind that nothing would spoil the moment. "Try it on," I urged.

The sweater fit him perfectly, and it brought out the blue in his eyes better than I'd imagined. He was going to be the heartthrob of Vail. But for the moment I didn't care. He was ecstatic, and he just kept looking in the hall mirror, saying he didn't believe it. "Look at these racing stripes. I look like a real hotdogger."

In spite of the fact that he was wearing a heavy shirt and the house was hot, Steve made no effort to take the sweater off. I could tell he was really happy with the present.

A moment later Steve fumbled in his pants pocket, drawing out a tiny box wrapped in silver foil. "Merry Christmas," he said.

My fingers were like icicles. I could barely manage to open the paper. Taking the lid off the box, I saw a gold locket on a chain. It was beautiful. Steve took it from the box and turned me toward him. Reaching around my neck, he fastened the locket. "Steve," I began, "I hardly know what to say—"

"Then don't say anything." He bent and kissed me tenderly. We went into the kitchen to make some hot chocolate, but every few seconds I reached up to touch the locket. *See, dummy, I lectured myself, he'd never have bought this if he didn't really care about you. Heather can't be all that important.* I felt a weight lift from my chest. For the first time, I could wish Steve a wonderful trip and mean every word of it. I told him that I knew I'd been acting a little weird and I was sorry.

A broad smile crossed Steve's face. "I'm so glad you told me that! You've been so—well, I just haven't known what to say to you. I wish more than anything that you could go with me."

I reached out to take his hand, feeling that things were finally right between us again. But Steve shied away. "Michelle, I don't know what's the matter with me. I shouldn't have said that. I'm just rubbing it in that I'm going and you're not. I'm really sorry." He sighed. "I talked to Heather today about how much I'm going to miss you, and she said that no matter what you said, the only fair thing to do was to make you promise to have a good time over vacation. Go ahead and go to parties and go out with—"

I started to protest that I didn't want to go to any parties without him, but Steve put his finger to my lips. "No arguing. It's only fair. And don't feel guilty. I mean I'm sure there are going to be parties and stuff up at Vail, too."

"But, Steve—" I started to explain.

Again he cut me off. "Michelle, I've really been thinking about this. Everything Heather said makes perfect sense. It's not right for you to be home alone all vacation, and it's not right for me to take my grandmother's money for the ski trip and then not enjoy it. So while I'm up at Vail, I'm going to go out and have fun. And I want you to have fun, too." He swallowed hard. "It won't be that long until we're together again. Everything will be fine, I know it will."

So far Heather had done a great job of ruining

everything, and the trip hadn't even started yet. I wondered just what Steve would consider "fine" by the time the trip was over.

Chapter Six

The evening grew worse. The more I tried to convince Steve that I didn't want to go out without him, the more defensive he acted.

Finally he said, "Well, I guess we should call it a night. You're probably beat from working all day, and I've got to get up at six in the morning to leave." His kiss good night lacked any real feeling, and I was sure that he was slipping out of my life before he'd even left the house.

After Steve had gone, I sat in my room replaying our goodbye. His parting words had been that Klausner's was lucky to be getting such a terrific salesperson and I should be proud of having gotten the job. He'd made no mention of missing me or sending me postcards from Vail. It was as if I were already a part of the past.

I woke up Monday morning still feeling miserable. At least I was working, which would be better than sitting at home thinking about Steve and Heather on the slopes together. I pulled off my nightgown and quickly dressed. The gold locket looked great with the sweater I was wearing. I wondered whether it was a token of Steve's love or a salve for his conscience for dumping me.

The day was gray, and the cold cut right through my coat as I waited for the bus downtown. I carried my shoes in a plastic bag and wore boots to climb through the dirty snow. Fortunately the bus was five minutes early, and there was even an empty seat. I hoped both things were good omens for the day. As the bus travelled its familiar route, I decided it would be fun to work in ski accessories again. I liked Mr. Holden, and I almost knew where to find everything in the department.

The bus reached my stop, and it was no time before I was pushing the door open to Klausner's. After pinning on my name tag, I reported to Jane. "Ah, Ms. Gunderson, good morning!" she said when I reached the front of the line.

"Am I back in ski accessories?" I asked.

She checked her computer printout. "No, I'm sorry. But you'll love your new assignment. We're sending you to the toy department. As you probably know, your shift will be over at five with a lunch break around one-thirty."

I made my way to the toy department, feeling excited about working there. I'd enjoyed selling ski accessories, but what could be more fitting at Christmas than selling toys? I thought of the year that I was seven. I'd wanted a Barbie doll more than anything. During the weeks just before Christmas, I'd pulled my mom into every toy department I saw. I kept telling her that, just in case Santa was watching, I wanted him to know which Barbie I wanted.

I'd know soon enough which toy was the rage for seven-year-old girls this year, I thought, I walked off the escalator and under the huge candy-cane arch that stood in front of the toy department.

Staring up at the candy canes, I felt the same tingling excitement that I'd felt when I was younger. *Christmas really is for kids,* I told myself, but my thoughts were suddenly interrupted by a voice behind me.

"You the lamb that got sent to slaughter this week?"

I turned to see a very thin woman with her gray hair tightly pulled into a bun. "Last week's temp probably quit before she'd come back to this department again. I swear, we ought to get medals for working here at Christmas."

Another lady looked out from one of the aisles. "Oh, Ann, it's not so bad." Then she chuckled. "Of course, it *is* a little like getting caught in the middle of a hurricane." She walked over to me. "Hi, I'm Millie," she said, extending her hand. "This is Ann, the toy department's resident

Scrooge." She went on almost without taking a breath. "I was just trying to restock a few of the Cabbage Patch accessories before the crowd hits."

Just then Klausner's was officially open for business. I started to unpack one of the boxes at Millie's feet. "Anything special I should know?"

Millie laughed and said, "Expect anything, it'll probably happen."

Forty-five minutes later I, who rarely baby-sat, was holding a screaming baby for a mother who was seeing if her toddler was the right size for a small riding toy.

"What do I do?" I called to the mother above the baby's screams.

"Try bouncing him a little. I've just got to see whether Bobby can keep his balance on the wooden duck." At last she took the baby from my arms.

"I want it, Mommy," whined the toddler. "Please, please, please!" My head was beginning to hurt.

"Now, Bobby, we'll just have to put it on the list for Santa," she said sternly. As soon as the child turned away, the mother whispered to me, "Here's my charge. Could you ring it up in a hurry and put it in a bag so Bobby doesn't see it?"

When I stepped behind the counter, Millie was ringing another lady's purchases—all ten of them—so I had to wait to use the register. As I waited, the baby screamed and Bobby whined. I had finally finished charging the toy when I discovered that the Ride-Along-Ducky was bigger than any of our bags. Taping three bags together, I finally concealed the toy and handed it to the mother. Bobby left the department glancing backward longingly at the Ride-Along-Ducky display. His mother turned to wave and call thanks to me. In spite of the bedlam, I smiled, thinking of Bobby opening his present on Christmas morning.

An elderly man tapped me on the shoulder. He said he was puzzled by his grandson's list. Where and what, he wanted to know, were He-Man and Skeletor? I wasn't too sure myself because I hadn't really had time to get to know the department. I assured the man that I'd find the toys for him.

I'd gotten about three steps down one aisle when a lady grabbed me. "I'm about to drop this," she said, holding an enormous stuffed animal. "And I can't find anyone to ring it up."

I told her I'd be right with her and took about three more steps before a woman asked me where the Cabbage Patch accessories were. By the time I'd pointed out the section, I'd forgotten what the old man had wanted me to find.

Still, in spite of the chaos and tumult, there was an air of holiday excitement that was special. It was a lot of fun to see all the new toys that had come out since I was little.

The toy department was very crowded the whole day. It seemed that the fewer toys we had, the more frantic parents became. I worked without stopping until my shift ended.

Exhausted, I got my coat, checked out, then made my way out the heavy glass doors onto the icy sidewalks. The cold was biting, and there were so many people at the stop that I didn't see how we'd ever all fit on the bus. By the time I got home, I was more than ready to sink into a hot bath.

As I lay in the tub absorbing its warmth, I finally had time to think about Steve and Heather. But Mom knocked on the bathroom door interrupting me. "Dinner's about ready, and you've been in the tub long enough to have turned into a wrinkled prune."

"I'm coming," I called back. I got out of the tub and put on my pink terry cloth robe. Mom called me again, and I started down the stairs. Just as I reached the bottom step, I heard Scott asking Mom, "How come if I'm late, I always get in trouble, but Michelle can show up for dinner whenever she wants?"

I walked into the kitchen and glared at Scott. Boys, whether brothers or boyfriends, seemed to exist only to make life miserable.

Chapter Seven

When I got to work the next day, I found I'd been moved to another department. I stopped by toys to tell Ann and Millie goodbye. I would have liked to continue working with them.

"I wish they hadn't moved me," I said regretfully.

Millie shook her head good-naturedly. "I'm not surprised; I'll bet they're putting you in fragrances, jewelry, or lingerie. Those departments are always the busiest ones the last few days before Christmas."

"You're right," I said. "I'm going to be in ladies' costume jewelry on the main floor." Ann and Millie wished me luck, and I started back down to the first floor. Being a "temp" was interesting, but I didn't think I'd like to do it for too long. Every time I began to get my bearings, I got transferred to a new department.

It seemed strange, after moving around the

ski accessories and toy departments, to be stuck behind one counter. And after handling large stuffed animals and bulky ski gloves and boots, I felt funny wrapping rings, necklaces, and bracelets in tissue so they wouldn't get lost in the smallest bags available.

Since the jewelry department was near the front of the store, people streamed by it to get into the rest of Klausner's many departments. Standing behind the counter, watching the package-laden crowds pour in and out, was really interesting. People of every description came into Klausner's. Mothers wrestled with bags and boxes and still managed to hang on to bundled-up children. Men strode purposefully toward the cosmetics and perfume counters, then looked helpless once they arrived. Couples held hands and pointed to the large wreaths overhead. Some of them looked so in love that I couldn't help wondering what Steve was doing right then. Was he with Heather?

There was a steady but not overwhelming business in jewelry. Sometimes the people were funny. They'd bring me two rings and ask me which one I thought their aunt might like better. At first I tried to explain that since I didn't know their aunt, I couldn't possibly say. Then I realized that they were just tired and confused. I could make things a lot easier on both of us if I just picked out whichever ring I personally liked better.

I found a necklace with matching pierced earrings that I really loved. I thought they'd be great Christmas presents for Mom, but we weren't allowed to ring up our own purchases. There didn't seem to be anyone available who could do it for me. I turned around for just a minute to safely stash the necklace and earrings behind the counter when I saw exactly what they had warned us to look for in our security briefing. A man casually picked up a handful of bracelets and stuffed them into the pocket of his coat.

For an instant I stood frozen to the spot. Could I really have seen what I thought I'd seen? It had to be. But what was I supposed to do? My hands began trembling, and I knew I'd have to act fast or it would be too late. My mind went blank. I could picture the red-headed security lady who'd lectured us during the training session, but I couldn't think what she'd said. Finally some of her words popped into my head, and I moved to the phone to dial thirty-one.

"Security," said a voice at the other end.

"Uh," I said, barely hearing my own voice, "I'm in jewelry. This man, he just took some bracelets." I could feel my heart pounding and my head throbbing. The rest of the crowd became a blur as I tried to keep the man in view while I talked to security. I knew I wasn't following procedure, but I couldn't remember exactly what I was supposed to say.

"Which jewelry?"

"Ladies costume."

"Can you describe the suspect?"

"Uh—"

"Give us some idea how we might identify him," the voice prompted.

"He's—he's stopped at another counter closer to the doors."

The voice started to sound angry. "Tell me what he's wearing."

"He's wearing a red ski parka." My voice was cracking. There were probably lots of men in the crowd wearing red parkas. "And, uh, he's—uh, kind of fat, and he has black hair."

At the counter an older woman in a fur coat was calling me. "Miss, miss, I'm really in a hurry. Can't you take that phone order later and ring these things up for me now?"

By the time I'd given the best description I could, the man was at the last counter next to the store entrance. He was going to get away with all that jewelry, and it was my fault. If only I'd remembered what I was supposed to do faster and better. There was no way store security would reach him in time. Suddenly I had an idea.

I locked my register and walked quickly from behind the counter. The woman who'd been calling for my help looked amazed and then furious as she saw me heading for the store exit. Trying not to appear too out of breath, I caught up with the man just before he'd gotten out of the first set of doors.

"Excuse me," I said, forcing a smile. "I'm a Klausner's personal shopper. We're new this Christmas season, and we're here to make certain you don't leave Klausner's without finding what you want."

The man tried to ignore me and keep walking. "Please," I said. "I see you have no packages, so you must not have found what you wanted. I really could help you. At least let me try."

"No, thanks," he mumbled as he shoved past me. I stood where I was, watching him push through the crowd moving closer to the heavy glass doors that would assure his escape back into the crowds on Sixteenth Street.

He disappeared through the first set of doors. He'd shoplifted, and he'd gotten away with it because of my stupidity. It was just that simple. They'd probably fire me. And who could blame them? I trudged slowly back toward the jewelry counter. If only there hadn't been so much to learn in that training session. If only the part about store security hadn't come at the very end when I was already so tired. If only there'd been another employee who'd seen him shoplift. I got back to my jewelry counter and walked behind it.

"Say," said a customer, "could you suggest something for my child's music teacher?"

I looked around the counter. The fur-coated woman who'd been calling me while I was on the phone with security was gone. Lying on the counter were the necklaces she'd planned to buy. The customer in front of me repeated herself. "Do you think a music teacher would like a necklace or a bracelet better?"

I shook my head to clear my thoughts. I'd lost enough money for Klausner's that day, I knew I'd better help this woman. Still, there was something amazing about the way everything continued as if nothing had happened. I had half expected bells to go off and people to scream. "I, uh, well, we have a pin in the shape of a piano, how about that?"

The woman seemed pleased. "That's a great idea. I'll take it." I had just finished ringing up the woman's purchases and putting away the necklaces the lady in the fur coat had left when the phone rang.

"Ladies' costume jewelry," I answered.

"Is this the employee who reported the shoplifting?"

Feeling a rising sense of dread, I said that it was. The person at the other end curtly informed me that someone would be coming to relieve me. As soon as she arrived, I was requested to report to security. Actually it didn't sound much like a request at all. It sounded a lot more like an order.

As I hung up, I noticed a guy who looked like he was in college leaning up against the counter. He was browsing through the bracelets. He kept casting glances at me and then at the bracelets, and a sixth sense told me he wasn't going to buy anything. Wearing beat-up old jeans and a sweat shirt, he was carrying a blue parka over one arm and holding a small shopping bag. Under normal circumstances, I might have even thought he was cute, but all I could think of was *Oh, no, it just can't be another shoplifter.* I hurried over to him, hoping if I got there soon enough he wouldn't take anything.

I put on a smile even though I was shaking in my shoes. "Those are nice bracelets, can I help you with one?"

He waited until I was directly across from him, and then he grinned. "That's pretty funny. I just stopped by to tell you that you did some real quick thinking. I don't know how you stalled him, but it worked."

I was lost. Who was this guy, and what was going on? I looked at him dumbly. "What?"

His voice dropped almost to a whisper. "I'm store security. We got the guy."

"You did?" I shouted with disbelief.

He looked uncomfortable. "Well, thanks, anyway," he said. "I don't think those bracelets are quite what my girlfriend would like. I may keep them in mind if I don't find anything else, though." With that he blended into the crowd and was gone. In a million years I'd never have picked him out as a security guard. In fact, I still couldn't quite believe what he'd said.

How could they have gotten the shoplifter? He had almost left the store. I'd seen him with my own eyes; no one had stopped him. And if they had gotten him, why the stern voice requesting that I come to security? I wished that the relief salesperson would hurry up. The suspense was killing me.

I didn't realize that an elderly woman had walked up to the counter. Now that I thought about it, she'd been there for a few minutes. Had that been why the security guard had changed the conversation so quickly? I just couldn't keep up with all this.

"Listen, dear," she said, interrupting my thoughts, "I'd really love to get some of these earrings that are shaped like Christmas wreaths, especially at this wonderful sale price, but my hands shake so badly these days. Do you think if I bought them, you could put them through the holes in my ears?"

"Well," I said doubtfully, "I could try."

"Oh, bless you," she said, paying for the earrings. I found my own hands shaking a bit. What if I stabbed her in the ear? Fortunately the earrings slid right in, and the woman was profuse in her thanks. She walked away wishing me a very Merry Christmas and a wonderful New Year.

The floater finally arrived to relieve me. As I took my purse from behind the counter, I felt my knees begin to shake. Suddenly I wished I could send the floater to security in my place.

When I got downstairs, I reported to the woman on duty, and she sent me to a room. The same lady who'd given the lecture at the training session was there, and I wondered if she was about to go through it all again for the dumb one in the class—me.

Actually she told me that when the man had been arrested, not only did he have the five bracelets from my department, but a number of other things as well. It seemed that the "fat" I'd described was Klausner merchandise he'd hidden inside his coat. His parka had had all kinds of special interior pockets. He'd taken a calculator, a couple of pen-and-pencil sets, and a gold belt. The security lady looked grim as she said that he'd even managed to conceal an expensive suede sports coat and two shirts under his parka. "It appears he was doing his Christmas shopping without bothering to pay for it," she said. In all, he had accumulated over seven hundred dollars worth of merchandise from six different departments. She continued, "And you were the only salesperson who noticed him." She reminded me to call more quickly in the future with a better description. "I'm curious about something. They told me that you managed to stall him and keep him in the store until the security people spotted him. Whatever did you say to him?"

I told her what I'd said and done. I didn't tell

her I had no idea that security had picked up on the guy before he left the store.

The woman told me more about Klausner's security operation, and I found myself fascinated. I knew that given the choice, I'd much rather work there than in sales. Still, I didn't think I'd better push my luck by asking about it that day. Mrs. Glick, the woman in charge of security, dismissed me and told me that I had time to stop in the employee cafeteria for a break before I reported back to the floor.

An hour before, I'd been sure I was going to get fired. Instead, I'd been commended on having sharp eyes. I'd spotted a shoplifter that people in five other departments had missed. Pushing through the doors to the employee cafeteria, I wished I could have seen his parka. I wondered if he had sewn all the special interior pockets into the coat himself or if there was some place that thieves could go to buy such things.

I got myself a Coke and sat down to drink it. I wished I'd see the security guy who looked like a college student again. There sure were lots of questions I wanted to ask him. I strained to remember Mrs. Glick's initial security lecture. As I recalled, she'd said there were two types of security people in the store—uniformed and plain clothes. The college guy was obviously plain clothes. I wondered if he wore jeans every day or if he changed his look often. Suddenly it occurred to me that some of these nice, normal-looking people sitting in the cafeteria with me must be with store security.

I took a sip of my Coke and imagined the dinner table conversation that evening. Mom would ask me how work had gone. Scott would groan and mumble that he wished we didn't always have to talk about my being a salesperson. Well, wait until he heard about my day. I could almost picture the look of surprise and envy on his face.

Chapter Eight

Thank goodness the rest of the day was uneventful. Sitting at the dinner table that night, I felt as if I were about to burst. I took a helping of mashed potatoes and listened to Dad telling Mom about some business deal he was working on. When he finished, he asked, "Well, princess, how was your day?"

I didn't say anything for a minute, and just as I had predicted, Scott groaned and said, "Do we have to always—" Dad fixed him with a warning look, and Scott stopped midsentence.

With deliberate casualness, I said, "Well, as a matter of fact, I had a very interesting day. I caught a shoplifter."

For a minute there was silence around the table, as if no one knew quite what to say. Then Scott burst forth excitedly, "Wow, did you chase him? Did he try to shoot you?"

My mother stopped him. "Scott, calm down and let your sister tell us what happened."

The whole family listened as I retold the story. It was fun being the center of attention.

Throughout the evening I thought about the store's security. I decided that the next day, I'd keep careful watch and see if I could figure out who some of the plainclothes people were.

Later, as I was falling asleep, I wished I could share my news with Steve. It was only ten o'clock, and I wondered what he was doing right then. I had checked the mail that day as soon as I came home, hoping there'd be a postcard from him. Of course, there had been nothing. Deep down, I knew there wouldn't be any. He wasn't going to write, and he wasn't going to care about me the way he used to when he came back. I kept telling myself so, trying to make it sink in. I wanted to be prepared when Steve came home and told me it was over, but my mind and my heart just couldn't get together. It didn't matter how much my head told me to forget him. My heart said that I missed him tremendously and wished desperately that everything would be OK.

When sleep finally came, I had another jumbled, twisted dream. I was the head of store security at a big department store. Heather walked in, carrying an oversize, blue, knitted bag, which she began to fill with merchandise. I watched, and when she'd finished stuffing ski outfits into it, she headed for the exit. I grabbed her and gleefully told her that she was going to jail forever. It seemed that I'd been especially lucky because the president of the store had witnessed my quick action, and I was sure he was coming to congratulate me on my efficiency. He began walking toward me, but I couldn't quite see his face until he was right in front of me. It was a gray-haired version of Steve. He looked furious and ordered me not to bother Heather ever again; he said she could do whatever she wished.

When I woke up the next morning, I felt tired. No wonder. What a crazy dream. I dressed for work, and slipping on my black pumps, I remembered how much they'd hurt the first day I'd worn them. Either I'd broken them in, or I'd just gotten used to being on my feet eight hours a day.

I'd been told that I'd be staying in costume jewelry through Christmas Eve, so I punched in and reported directly to my department. About eleven a familiar-looking boy wandered by the counter. He toyed with a bracelet, looked at a couple of the Christmas pins, then wandered away. A short while later he returned. I hoped he wouldn't take off again before I finished with my customer. As soon as the customer walked away, I hurried over to the boy. "You look so different. Tell me who you're watching today," I asked eagerly.

He smiled at me and said, "You." I began to

blush, and his grin told me he'd noticed. "I figured if you're going to do my job so well, maybe I'd better learn how to do yours." I blushed even more furiously and was sure that the color of my face matched my red blouse. Too embarrassed to ask him any more questions, I looked at him in silence. He winked and then walked away.

As he sauntered off, I decided that if he came back, I'd be the one ready with a clever retort. I'd see how he liked to be the one who was embarrassed. But before I could figure out something to say to him, the counter was crowded with customers again. These last-minute Christmas shoppers had a whole different attitude from the ones who had come in even a few days earlier. There was a desperate quality about them. They didn't seem too particular about what they bought, as long as they could cross another name off their Christmas lists. Mixed in with the late shoppers were a few people who were already beginning to return gifts they'd received early. In fact, the last transaction I handled before lunch was a lady who was returning two bracelets. She said they'd been a gift from her son, who wouldn't be able to be with her on Christmas.

I told her I was sorry to hear that. I hoped that she couldn't hear the loud grumblings of my hungry stomach. I could hardly wait for lunch.

By the time I got to the employee cafeteria, it was almost one-forty. I was so hungry, I was ready to ask for one of everything! I went through the line, picking out a salad and vegetable soup; I even splurged on a big wedge of chocolate cake. I carried my tray toward the tables, looking to see if Mr. Holden or Millie or even Ann was around. It wasn't much fun to eat lunch alone. Unfortunately I didn't see any of the few people I knew, so I put my tray down at one of the smallest tables and resigned myself to eating alone.

"Well, if it isn't the sleuth from ladies' costume jewelry," came a voice from behind me. I turned around to see the boy from security. He put his tray on my table. "It's bad for your digestion to eat by yourself."

When I didn't protest, he sat down and began unloading two hamburgers, a milk shake, an order of fries, and a piece of cake similar to my own.

Seeing me watch the amount of food he was setting down, he winked and said, "Hey, we good guys have to make sure we've got enough to eat. Can't catch the bad guys on an empty stomach."

"Right," I said. "Does this good guy have a name?"

He said that his name was Don Neher and he was working in store security just for the Christmas break while he was home from college. I told him that I thought store security must be much more interesting than sales, and he laughed. "It's not all running after shoplifters. We do a lot of inventory investigation and a lot of paper-work. Still, it isn't too bad."

The conversation flowed easily, and I couldn't believe how fast my lunch hour passed. I hated to have to leave. Don seemed to enjoy my company, too, because the last thing he said to me before I took off was, "Tell you what. Why don't I stop by your department tomorrow and find out what time your lunch hour is? If you want, we could eat together again."

"That'd be great," I said, and I meant it. Of course, Don wasn't Steve, and I didn't feel that wonderful fluttery feeling when he was around. But he sure was nice and lots of fun to talk to. Also, it made me feel good that he was a college sophomore and wanted to spend time with me. As I put my purse back under the counter and prepared to wait on people, I realized that I was really looking forward to my lunch hour the next day.

I kept an eye out for Don all afternoon, hoping he'd stop by my department. I had to remind myself to look for a well-dressed guy. His grubby look of the day before had given way to a very preppie one. His sandy brown hair was neatly combed, and his large brown eyes looked very serious behind large tortoiseshell glasses. Some-how, in his blue pin-striped shirt, green V-neck sweater, and navy slacks, he even looked taller. There was no way that a casual observer would ever have realized that he was the same person who'd been in the store the day before. During lunch he'd told me that the store's plainclothes detectives altered their appearances frequently. They were even moved from store to store so that shoppers wouldn't recognize them. He'd laughed. "Wait until you see me in my cowboy outfit. I look as if I've come right off the ranch."

The store sound system was playing "It's Beginning to Look a Lot Like Christmas," but it was already beginning to seem as if Christmas were over. Memos had been circulated on handling gift returns and the special hours for the after-Christmas sales. Much as I loved the holiday season, I couldn't say that I'd be sorry to hear the Christmas carols end. They played all day, every day, and I was beginning to get a little sick of them. Even my favorite, "Silent Night," was starting to get on my nerves. But the next day was Christmas Eve, and I supposed I could stand the music for one more day.

To my disappointment the afternoon passed and Don never came anywhere near ladies' costume jewelry. It had seemed to me that he was flirting at lunch, but maybe he just didn't like eating alone and didn't know too many people at the store either.

When I walked in the house that evening, Scott practically knocked me down. "Well, who'd you capture today?" he asked excitedly. "No one," I said, but I couldn't resist baiting him. "I did have lunch with a store security agent, though."

"Wow, neato. What'd he say?" Scott exclaimed.

"Oh, I can't tell you," I said in a stern voice. "It's kind of confidential, if you know what I mean." I climbed the stairs toward my room. I'd just scored one for my side in the ongoing battle with my little brother.

I smiled to myself thinking that even though Scott drove me nuts, I really did love him. In fact, I was glad that I'd gotten him such a terrific Christmas present. Guiltily I remembered that mine were the only gifts not already under our tree. I'd been so busy that I hadn't even wrapped one present yet.

I went into my room, shut the door, and pulled out my family's gifts and one roll of silver and one of red wrapping paper from under my bed. I wrapped my mother's package first. I was sure she would like the necklace and earrings I'd gotten her. Dad had been a lot harder to shop for. I'd used two of my breaks and one lunch hour to find the perfect present for him. I really wasn't sure I'd succeeded. Looking for something unusual, I had passed up the button-down shirt and the socks he'd hinted he wanted. Finally, running out of time and ideas, I'd selected a big book on the history of golf. Golf was Dad's favorite hobby. But as I wrapped his present, I kept thinking that playing the game was what he enjoyed, I didn't really know whether he'd like reading about it. I made an elaborate bow for his package. At least I could make sure that he liked the way his present was wrapped. Finally, I pulled out Scott's sweater. Before I put it in the box, I held it up. It really was beautiful; it was made of heavy, finely woven wool. Though I had tried everything to keep from thinking of Steve, I couldn't look at Scott's sweater without seeing Steve in his. He had looked so handsome in it the last night we'd been together. I wondered if he'd been wearing it much while he skied. Had it kept him warm? Had it made him think of me at all? I sighed, thinking those might be questions to which I'd never hear the answers.

I was jarred from my thoughts by Scott's shrill scream. "Michelllllle, Mom wants you to come down for dinner." The voice got louder, and it sounded as if Scott was right outside my room.

"Don't come in here," I yelled. "I'll be there in a minute." I put the sweater in the box and stuffed it under my bed again. I'd have to finish wrapping it after dinner.

Chapter Nine

"Hey," one employee called out as we walked into the store the next morning, " 'tis the day before Christmas."

Another responded, laughing, "And all through the store it's only a few hours till we close the doors."

"Not bad," said the first. "Not bad at all." And both of them began walking downstairs to check in for work. Maybe it was because we were closing early or maybe it was just that Christmas Eve always brought the best out in people, but the mood in the store was very festive.

There was a sign on the employee bulletin board that said the cafeteria would be serving complimentary eggnog and cookies throughout the day to thank everyone for his or her hard work. We had also been requested to leave our departments in spick-and-span order; longtime employees said that it was impossible to survive the day-after-Christmas sales if you didn't. Since business was somewhat sporadic, I rearranged the display cases to cover bare spots and cleared the countertops for returns. I kept an eye out for Don, but didn't see him once. In fact, I began to wonder if he'd been transferred to another store for the day. I hoped he'd show up soon. If he still wanted to eat with me, he better hurry. I'd been assigned the early lunch.

By eleven-thirty Don still hadn't come by my department, and I couldn't wait any longer. I made my way to the cafeteria with regret. It would have been nice to have had lunch with him, but there was nothing I could do. The cafeteria was unusually full. While waiting in line, I mentioned that to the person behind me, and she laughed. "It just goes to show that if you offer people something for free, everyone turns up." Passing by the main dishes I didn't feel very hungry. I picked out a glass of iced tea and a salad. As I reached the cash register, I took out my wallet.

"I'll get that," said a deep voice from behind me.

"That's a dollar ninety," said the cashier. After Don paid her, he took the tray from my hands. "I'm sitting over there," he said, gesturing.

I said, "You didn't have to pay for my lunch, and how'd you know what time my lunch hour was, anyway?"

"Listen, I asked you to lunch. Did you think I'd stand you up?" He smiled.

Over lunch he explained that he'd been very busy with a rather complicated shoplifting. Knowing he wouldn't have time to stop by my department, he'd asked a friend to check the lunch schedules. Just as it had the day before, conversation flowed easily. I found myself telling him about our move from Tucson and how hard it had been to leave all my old friends. He said that I'd probably be surprised to discover that, if I ever went back, I wouldn't have much in common with those friends. Almost all of his friends were from UCLA now, and he said he had barely kept in touch with his high-school buddies. "It's funny how things change after you've been away for a while," he added thoughtfully. "You're never quite the same person you once were." For just an instant Steve's face flashed across my mind. I fought a sudden urge to ask Don if he thought a few days could cause such a change. Of course, I didn't ask him.

Don told me about life at UCLA, and I thought it sounded like a terrific place to go to college. He also told me he had to work very hard to help his parents with the costs. "I know the extra costs are hard on them," he told me. "So I've been trying to contribute as much as I can. I was kind of counting on working in construction last summer because it pays so well, but then Denver hit a building slump. There were no construction jobs available. In fact, the job market was pretty tight all over. It looked like I wasn't going to be able to contribute a penny to my education. One night I was talking on the phone to my older brother in Omaha. I complained that I was having trouble finding a summer job, and he suggested that I apply to Klausner's. He'd worked in security here when he was in college. So that's what I did. At first they said they weren't hiring either. But then they called and said that if I was as good as my brother, they'd give me a try. I worked here last summer, and that's why I'm back now." Don smiled at me and shrugged. "So that's my whole story. Now let me guess why they hired you. The head of personnel saw a pretty girl with beautiful blue eyes and said to himself, 'Hmm, I'll bet people would like to buy things from her.' "

I laughed. "Not quite. I begged and pleaded and then crossed my fingers and waited until they finally needed more Christmas help."

"I like my version a lot better," he said lightly.

He was a lot more sophisticated than any of the high-school boys I knew. I was sure that most of what he was saying was a line, but it was fun anyway. We talked some more about school and shoppers and security. In no time I had to head back to my department. After thanking Don for lunch, I left the cafeteria and went down the escalator. I thought about Don as I walked. *Well*, I asked myself angrily, *how can you care so much about Steve and still enjoy flirting with Don?*

I wasn't really flirting. We were just talking, said a part of me in defense.

Right, I argued back. *Then how come you hope he shows up in your department this afternoon?* I didn't have an answer.

About an hour before closing, the display department began hanging up red and white After-Christmas Sale signs. To make room for them, some of the Christmas decorations were already being removed. Christmas was ending at Klausner's before Christmas Day had even dawned. The phone rang, and it was personnel asking if the girl at the next counter could cover for me for a few minutes. They wanted me to come down and get my schedule for the next week.

The crowds had all gone home except for a few harried stragglers. I could feel everyone's anxiety to close the store and go home for Christmas Eve. In personnel, Jane told me that they definitely wanted to schedule me for full-time work during the next week. "Will I be in jewelry again?" I asked.

Jane checked her computer. "I'm afraid not," she said. "Our clothing departments are going to be much busier. We'll put you in ladies' sportswear and see how it goes from there." I started to leave, but Jane stopped me. "Oh, I almost forgot, Mrs. Glick wants to see you. Let me buzz her and see if she's available now."

In a minute I was sitting across a desk from the red-jacketed head of security. "Michelle," she said, smiling, "I always like to make these presentations in person. We thank you again for your help." With that she handed me a long white envelope.

"What's this?" I asked, confused.

"Open it," she said brightly. I did so, and there was a check inside for twenty-five dollars. "When one of our employees, except of course those in security, is responsible for identifying a shoplifter, we want to make sure they know it's appreciated. The check is our way of saying thank you."

As I walked back up to my department, I took the check out to look at it again and thought to myself, *Well, Merry Christmas to you, Michelle Gunderson.* Soon after I returned to the jewelry department, I saw a familiar figure walk past the counter. It seemed as if Don were going to stop and talk, but he kept walking. A few minutes later he was back again. "Sir," I called for the benefit of anyone listening. "Could I help you with something?"

He grinned and walked up to the necklaces in front of me. "Well, now that you mention it, you probably can."

"Good," I said in my most professional voice. "How can I help?"

His brown eyes appraised me slowly. "Well, you could go out with me New Year's Eve."

His words caught me off guard. I had expected him to make some joke about looking for a bracelet or earrings or something. Not knowing what else to do, I decided to just ignore his comment.

"The necklace isn't quite what you were looking for," I said. "Perhaps I could show you one of our bracelets."

He put his elbows on the counter and appeared to be studying a necklace carefully. "That's not much of an answer." He looked up at me. "How about trying yes or no."

I wished I could think of something cute or clever to say, but all that popped out was, "Are you kidding?"

Don was beginning to look a little uncomfortable himself now. "No. I was asking you out for a date." A slow grin spread across his face. "Tell me, how do the other boys you know usually ask girls out?"

I thought immediately of Steve. Steve, who had tenderly kissed me and said that he couldn't imagine starting the New Year without me by his side. Of course, that had been almost a month ago. So much had changed since then. Was I really foolish enough to believe that Steve still planned to be with me on the best date night of the whole year?

Coming back to reality, I told Don that I'd have

to check on some other tentative plans I'd made. I asked if I could let him know after Christmas. He said sure and continued his patrol of the store.

I stood there in a daze as he walked away. Everything was so confusing. I was quite flattered to have been asked out by a college guy, but mostly I just wanted Steve to come home and tell me that he still cared. There was no doubt that Steve was the one I really wanted to be with on New Year's Eve. On the other hand, if he was going to dump me when he came back, it would be nice to have him think that I'd found someone else as well. Besides, Don was nice, and he was cute. If I couldn't be with Steve, at least I could go out and have fun with Don.

The closing bells finally sounded, and there was a spontaneous cheer. I was probably the only one in the entire store who trudged glumly out the door.

I tried to decide what to do about New Year's Eve for the entire bus ride home but couldn't come up with an answer. During our family's traditional singing of Christmas carols around the piano, I thought some more. And I was still thinking when I fell asleep.

I awakened early the next day to Scott's shouts. "It snowed. It really snowed on Christmas," he kept repeating. I forced my eyes open and walked to the window. Outside, it really was a fairyland. It must have snowed most of the night, and the sun was shining on a world of untouched whiteness, sending forth shimmers and sparkles. I sucked in my breath. Christmas in Tucson had never been anything like this.

After throwing on a robe, I ran downstairs to join my family. The drapes in the living room were wide open, and the lights of the Christmas tree blinked against the snowy scene outside. For a few minutes we all sat in silent awe. Then Dad built a big fire in the fireplace, and Mom went in to make hot chocolate. Breakfast could wait. We all still loved the excitement of opening our presents, and it wasn't long until the floor was littered with discarded wrapping paper, ribbons, and empty boxes. Dad seemed to be very interested in the book I'd gotten him. And as I'd hoped, Mom loved the jewelry. She jokingly asked how many times she was going to get to wear it before I borrowed it. But watching Scott open his present was the best of all. He let out a loud yell when he took it from the box and immediately pulled it on over his pajamas. I could tell that he liked the sweater almost better than anything else he'd gotten. That was saying a lot considering he was only ten and the sweater was clothing instead of a toy.

There was one big present and one little one left on the floor for me, and I was almost afraid to open the big one. For over a year I'd really wanted a stereo. The box looked about the right size, but I hated to open it and find out the gift was something else. I tried stalling, but everyone else had finished opening their presents.

So I tackled the big one, and within seconds I was screaming, "You did it! You really did it! You got me a stereo! Oh, thank you a zillion times." I ran over and hugged Mom and Dad. I was so excited that I was actually shaking.

"Now open mine," commanded Scott. I pulled off the wrapping to find an album I'd wanted for a long time. The family then went into the kitchen to eat a big breakfast of pancakes and bacon. Afterward I helped Mom with the dishes while Dad and Scott got out the projector to show home movies of past Christmases. It was a wonderful morning, and our midafternoon Christmas dinner was delicious. But by late afternoon, all the family's Christmas traditions were over for another year. Dad was engrossed in the book I'd gotten him. Scott had left for a friend's house to show off his new things, and Mom was chatting happily on the phone with my aunt Donna in Tucson. In spite of the heat from the fireplace, a cold loneliness crept through me. My thoughts were interrupted by a knock at the door.

I opened it to find Amy James, a friend from school. "I didn't get a chance to give you your Christmas present before I left," she said. "So I thought I'd drop it by today." I invited her in and went upstairs to get the present I'd bought for her. We sat on my bed talking about vacation and school. I really liked Amy, and I was glad she'd come over. She and her family had just returned from visiting relatives in California. I listened with envy as she told me about the beautiful beaches and assured her that her tan was going to be the envy of the whole school. Then Amy listened attentively as I told her all about what it was like to work at Klausner's. A couple of hours flew by before we'd both finished describing our vacation activities and there finally was a lull in the conversation.

"So what are you and Steve going to do for New Year's Eve?" she asked. I'd vowed not to discuss my problems with Steve with anyone until I had had a chance to figure out exactly how I felt. But it was as if she'd asked the right question at the right time. I guess that deep down I must have wanted to discuss it with someone because I answered Amy truthfully.

"Well," I said, in what I hoped was a very casual manner, "I'm not sure we're doing anything."

"Why not?" Amy asked in surprise.

"Well, I'm not so sure that Steve and I are still going to be seeing each other." It hurt to say the words aloud.

"Wow, you're kidding," she said. "What happened?"

I didn't tell her every gory detail. I just said that there could be some problems because

Steve and Heather were spending the whole vacation skiing together.

"You don't have to explain another thing," Amy responded. "I know just what you mean. They were the Ken and Barbie of the school before you came. I mean the two of them just looked as if they belonged together!" She realized what she'd said and put her hand over her mouth. "I'm sorry, Michelle, I didn't mean that you guys—"

"It's OK," I said, cutting her off. "Let's talk about something else."

Now Amy felt bad, and she tried to make things better. "Look," she said. "What do I really know anyway? I heard that Pam McCaul had to come home early from the ski trip because she broke her leg. Maybe I could call her, or you could call her and sound her out on what's been happening with Steve and Heather. Then you'd know whether you even had anything to worry about."

Maybe I could call her. It was a possibility. I started to wish I hadn't said anything about Steve. I'd been right in the first place. It was something I'd just have to work out on my own. Much as I liked Amy, when she finally said she had to get going, I was relieved. I had a lot of thinking to do.

Chapter Ten

After Amy left I sat in my room, staring at the phone on my night table. Pulling the phone book from my drawer, I reasoned that it couldn't possibly hurt to try to find Pam's number, although there were probably a lot of McCauls listed. To my surprise, however, there were only four listings under McCaul, and three of them lived too far away to be Pam.

Nervously I picked up the phone and dialed the number. It rang and rang. After the tenth ring, I put the phone back in its cradle. It was probably a stupid idea, anyway. Pam and I only knew each other because we'd been biology lab partners. How could I casually ask her about Steve and Heather?

But fifteen minutes later I was back at the phone. After all, Pam and I really had gotten along well in biology lab. Besides, the next day I had to give Don my answer about New Year's Eve and Pam was the only person who could help me with my decision. A voice answered on the second ring, and I calmly asked for Pam.

"Just a minute, I'll get her," said the voice, and the next thing I knew Pam picked up the phone.

"Hi and Merry Christmas," I said, feeling like an idiot and wishing I'd rehearsed just exactly what I wanted to say before I'd called. "This is Michelle Gunderson, and, uh, I heard that you broke your leg, and I called to say I was sorry," I said, rushing my words together.

"How great of you to call! And Merry Christmas to you, too," she exclaimed. "I've been so bored, and I'm sick of just sitting around. I still can't believe I broke my leg and ruined my whole trip. Anyway, I'm so glad you called. Did you have a good Christmas?"

Relieved that she was so friendly, I told her what I'd gotten and then told her about my job. It was fun to describe some of the crazy things that had happened at Klausner's. Still, I knew that somehow I had to get her to talk about the ski trip. The whole call would be wasted if I didn't find a way of asking her about Steve.

"Anyway, that's enough about me," I said lightly. "Tell me about the ski trip and how you broke your leg."

"Oh," she said, "I don't want to go through the whole thing again. It's too depressing to talk about it."

Terrific, I thought to myself. *Now what do I*

do? I can't make her talk about Steve. I'd already decided that if there was any chance that Steve might still care, I'd tell Don I couldn't go out New Year's Eve. I knew it was rude to bring up the ski trip after Pam had just said she didn't want to talk about it, but I had to forge ahead. Hoping she wouldn't get mad, I said, "Listen, I don't blame you for wanting to forget your whole trip, but I've got to ask you one question. You know Steve Johnson has kind of a bad knee"— that would be news to him—"and, uh, I heard that he was having trouble with it up at Vail. Is that true?"

Pam thought for a minute, but it seemed like hours to me. "A bad knee?" she said doubtfully. "Gee, he seemed just fine. Of course, I really don't know Steve too well. And since he's a great skier and I'm terrible, we weren't on the same slopes. As a matter of fact, he and Heather Lance took off for the advanced slopes every morning, and neither of them came down to the lodge for lunch."

Now that she'd started talking about it, Pam seemed eager to tell me a lot about her trip. She told me how miserable she felt about having to come home early. "Vail had to be the most per-fect, romantic spot in the whole world," she con-fided. She'd gone up to Vail with a tremendous crush on Bill Jenkins. Pam was sure that before the vacation was over, he'd ask her out. "Every night we had a big party—you know, come to think of it, Steve's knee must have been fine," Pam said. "He and Heather even won a dance contest." She continued by saying that she'd planned on being with Billy at every party. Instead, he was still up at Vail, and she was stuck at home.

We talked for a few minutes longer, and then Pam had to go and eat her Christmas dinner. She was so grateful that I called that I almost felt guilty for having an ulterior motive.

After hanging up, I stared at my reflection in the mirror. A rather longish face with two pleasant, but definitely not sexy, blue eyes stared back. "Well, Michelle Gunderson, you may not like what you heard, but you definitely got some answers."

My dad knocked on my door and asked to see me in his study. When I walked in, Scott was there, too. He had just gotten back from his friend's. "Listen, kids," Dad said. "Your mom is feeling pretty down. I think she really misses the big Christmas get-togethers in Tucson. Aunt Donna said on the phone that Grandma and Uncle Gary and Aunt Pat and the kids were all coming over to her house for dinner. I want you guys to help me keep Mom busy tonight so she isn't lonely." We agreed to help and spent Christmas evening playing Trivial Pursuit and Scrabble. No one went to bed until almost midnight. As I crawled exhausted into bed, I realized that for a few hours I'd stopped thinking of Steve and Heather.

I woke up late the next morning and made it to Klausner's barely in time. I put away my coat, punched in, and went right to ladies' sportswear. I'd been to lots of day-after-Christmas sales, but everything looked much different as an employee instead of a shopper. For one thing, employees couldn't decide that fighting the crowd wasn't worth it and go home. There also wasn't that feeling of excitement from getting a terrific buy. There was just a lot of hard work. I was stationed in front of a cash register in ladies' sportswear for the entire day. Above my head was a big sign that read Returns. I had been instructed as to what I could accept for cash return and what had to be taken for credit only. Sometimes I had to tell people that even though the merchandise was in a Klausner box, it wasn't ours and I couldn't take it back at all. By lunch I felt as if I'd been at work for ten hours, and I gratefully sank down in a chair in the cafeteria. It was then that I realized that I hadn't seen Don at all that day. I looked carefully around the cafeteria, but he was nowhere in sight. In fact, I didn't see him until about two in the afternoon. Out of the corner of my eye, I saw him approach my register wearing a baggy sweat shirt and a familiar grin. I certainly hoped he wasn't planning to ask me about New Year's Eve in front of all these people. I didn't want an audience. Don was now directly in front of me, and the woman who'd been first in line made a comment about people waiting their turn. He flashed a dazzling smile at her. "Sorry, ma'am, this is store business. It'll just take a minute, I promise, and thank you for shopping at Klausner's." He turned to me and stated loudly, "Ms. Gunderson, please make sure you take special care of Klausner's valuable customers." Then he whispered to me, "What time's your break?" I told him, and he said he'd meet me in the cafeteria.

After he left, the customer he'd edged in front of said that he seemed like a very nice young man. She did ask me why a store employee was dressed so shabbily. For a minute I was stumped. I knew I wasn't supposed to say that he was store security. "Uh, he's a buyer in this department, and today's his day off," I improvised. "He came in to make sure we'd marked the sweaters down."

When my break arrived, I could hardly wait to tell Don what had happened with that customer after he'd left. I knew he'd get a big kick out of the story that I'd invented. But by three-fifteen I'd been waiting in the cafeteria for ten minutes and Don hadn't shown up. My break was almost over when a woman who looked like my grandmother walked up to me. "Excuse me," she said. "Are you Michelle Gunderson?" When I told her I was, she handed me a note. "Don got very busy with something and asked me to give you this."

In the note he apologized for missing me and asked if I'd meet him after work. We certainly were having trouble catching up to each other. I wondered if it was a bad omen about New Year's Eve.

At five-thirty I grabbed my coat, clocked out, and went to the spot where Don had said he'd be. He stood lounging against a pillar. "Sorry about this afternoon. The least I can do is give you a ride home to make up for it," he said. The idea sounded wonderful. The day had been incredibly hectic, and I didn't feel much like fighting the crowds on the bus. We walked a couple of blocks to where Don had parked and climbed in a beautiful white Olds Cutlass.

"Nice car," I commented. He said that he thought so, too. It was his dad's, and he was only using it while he was home. "I've got an old junker at college. About half the time I have to have someone give me a push to get the thing started. I'd have driven it home, but I figured it would die on the trip." I laughed, and we talked about the day at work. In no time we were at my house, and suddenly I realized that nothing had been said about New Year's Eve. I wasn't sure whether I should bring it up or wait for Don to. Feeling somewhat awkward, I invited Don in, but he said he really had to get going. "Listen," he said, "they're sending me off to fight crime in the Cinderella City store for the rest of the week, so I probably won't be running in to you at work." He grinned. "In fact, maybe that's why they're sending me there, so I'll do my job instead of spending my time watching you."

I blushed. Don noticed my face reddening, and he seemed to enjoy my embarrassment. "So what do you think about New Year's Eve?"

I took a deep breath. *Darn you, Steve Johnson*, I thought angrily. Don was looking at me with one eyebrow raised quizzically. Finally I met his gaze and assured him that I'd love to go out with him on New Year's Eve.

"Great," he said. "I don't know what we'll do yet, but we should be able to find something that's fun. I'll check it out and give you a call."

"That sounds fine," I said. But nothing was fine, and I was sure it never would be again. With Steve and Heather starting the new year together, how could it be?

Don and I talked for a couple of minutes longer. As I started to open the car door, Don looked at me and grinned impishly. "Hey, supersleuth, I'm glad you decided to go." He winked. A date with Don definitely would not be dull.

Just once, I vowed, he wasn't going to tease me and then disappear after getting in the last word. So, I said back, "Tell you what. We can probably crack the case of who stole the old year."

101

I could feel Don's eyes appraising me as he slowly drawled, "I think we are going to have a very interesting evening."

With that the car roared away from the curb. I was left standing there, thinking that once again he'd managed to get in the final word.

Chapter Eleven

The after-Christmas sales continued at Klausner's on Monday in a hectic sort of way. One of our duties was to keep the dressing rooms clean, but it was almost impossible. In spite of a sign that clearly read "No more than four garments at a time," people took in however many things they wanted. For a while there was a woman checking people in and out of the dressing rooms, but she got transferred to another department. The store hadn't replaced her yet. The buyer came in and told us to keep as close an eye as possible on the dressing rooms, but that was pretty hard with everything else we had to do.

I'd just finished counting how many pairs of designer jeans we had left when a heavyset woman tapped me on the shoulder. She asked me if I worked there. When I told her that I did, she said, "Well, dear, I'm so sorry, but I believe

I've left your dressing room in quite a mess. You see I thought I wore a size ten, then I tried a size twelve. I guess manufacturers are cutting things pretty small because even the size fourteens seemed tight. Anyway, my watch stopped, and I just realized it. I'm very late for an appointment, so I can't clear out my dressing room. But I did want you to know that I'm sorry to leave things in such a state."

I watched her bustle off. Walking into the dressing rooms, I thought to myself that if she'd had time to tell me her whole story, she had had time to put the clothes back on the racks. In the dressing room hallway, I wondered which room had been the woman's. When I reached the last open door on the right, I gasped. No wonder this lady had taken off without putting anything back. She must have spent most of the morning creating the mess on the floor. I couldn't even see the carpet. Clothes completely covered it as well as the chair. At least twenty empty hangers were hanging from the three hooks on the walls. I had a sudden urge to just shut the door and leave the mess for someone else to deal with. Then my conscience got the better of me. I went out to the floor to tell my supervisor where I'd be and what I'd be doing and then started the job. I knew my mom would get a big kick out of this. At home she yelled at me for not putting away the skirt or sweater I'd worn to school, and there I was, picking up for a woman who'd probably spent the whole morning throwing clothes on the floor.

I'd put sixteen pairs of slacks back on hangers, and the room was still not straightened up. I had the feeling that I could spend the rest of the day in that dressing area. It was hard to believe that the woman had taken so many items in this room without our realizing she hadn't brought any of them back out.

As I worked, I heard two teenage girls enter the dressing room next to me. I was certain they had no idea I was there. If they had, I'm sure they wouldn't have appreciated my eavesdropping, but under the circumstances I could hardly avoid it. Besides, it made my job more enjoyable. At first the two of them talked about school and about some boy named Jim. Then one said she really loved the sweater the other was trying on. The second said, "I know it looks wonderful on me, it really does. But even on sale it's fifty dollars. I don't have that much money."

The conversation continued, and both of them decided that the sweater was just the thing the girl needed to catch Jim's attention. I almost wished that I could knock on their door and see the sweater myself. Instead, I had to make do with envisioning it. "You know," the first girl said, "why don't you just put the sweater in the bag with the other stuff you bought. No one will ever know the difference. Nobody pays any attention in these big stores. And, besides, it's not like you didn't buy other stuff here."

My heart started pounding. I didn't want to have to turn these girls in. When they were talking about Jim and about school, they sounded a lot like my friends and me. Still, I couldn't let them steal a sweater. But how could I stop them? I was too embarrassed to simply open the door to their dressing room and tell them I knew about their plan. Yet I knew that if I didn't do something fast, it would be too late. Quickly I left my dressing room and knocked on their door. A girl with long, sandy brown hair opened the door a crack. "Can I take any of the items you've decided you don't want?" I asked. "You know, we're trying not to let anyone have more than four garments in a room at a time."

The girl looked a little uncertain. "Look, it probably seems like a dumb rule," I went on, "but they're very careful around here about shoplifting. Boy, they arrested some kid the other day who was just about our age—"

Before I could say any more, the other girl, a short blond, handed me seven things. "Here," she said, and I could see that her hand was shaking. "We're really through anyway. You might as well take everything."

I thanked the girls, and as I walked back to the floor, I noticed that one of the items they had handed me was a sweater marked fifty dollars. I felt a sense of pride. I'd stopped them from shoplifting, and I hoped they'd been frightened enough not to think about doing it again. I wished Don were there. He'd really have appreciated the situation and the way I'd handled it. It was too bad that he was out in Cinderella City. Without Don my lunch hour and breaks would become rather lonely. In fact, I'd decided not to go down to the cafeteria for my breaks. Instead I'd spend them just wandering through the store looking for good buys.

I wasn't going to be too sorry to see this sales job end. I really liked earning money, but I just wasn't a true salesperson. Ms. Clark, the ladies' sportswear manager, had gotten very angry at me on Saturday because she didn't think I was trying hard enough to sell things. A customer had asked me if I thought a particular pink-and-white-striped blouse looked good with some gray slacks she was considering. I told her that it didn't look bad, but I thought she could do better if she kept looking. The woman agreed and ended up buying nothing from our department. Ms. Clark took me aside and gave me a lecture on selling.

I thought of Don with envy. If this job had taught me anything, it was that I was interested in the security aspect of retailing. Before I'd started at Klausner's, I hadn't ever given it any thought. I made up my mind that before I left, I'd see Mrs. Glick and ask if she'd consider me for a summer job in security. The thought was really exciting.

Ladies' sportswear stayed pretty busy. I sold a lot of clothes and handled lots of returns and exchanges. The days were long and hectic and went very quickly. In no time I was writing December twenty-ninth on sales slips and trying not to think that Steve was due home that day. *He'll call, I know he will*, I thought.

But then I decided he'd call to say we were breaking up. I involuntarily shuddered at the thought of receiving such terrible news. *Maybe, maybe, Steve was still planning to take me out for New Year's.* After all, how could one week with Heather make him forget the three perfect months we'd just spent together?

I decided that I was wrong to be so depressed that Steve hadn't written. After all, he went to Vail to go skiing, not to sit in his room writing letters. Maybe he hadn't sent me a postcard because he didn't want to make me feel bad about not being there. But then I knew I had to face facts: Steve hadn't written because he no longer cared. Nevertheless, in spite of everything, I held out a little hope that somehow everything would be OK.

When I got home from work that day, my hands felt a little shaky, and my heart was pounding. I tried to keep my voice calm as I asked Mom if there'd been any messages for me.

"No, dear," she said absently. "But I was out for part of the day."

At nine o'clock I was still waiting for the phone to ring. As I sat in the living room, I was torn between anger and worry. They'd been supposed to get in in the morning. I hoped he wasn't hurt, and I was furious that he hadn't called. When the phone finally rang at nine-thirty, I jumped and Scott ran for it. He got to the downstairs hall phone first. I could tell it was Steve because of Scott's enthusiastic greeting. From that point on, most of Scott's end of the conversation consisted of "Oh, wow. That's amazing." Pretty soon I was beginning to wonder if Steve was ever going to talk to me or if he was just planning to finish talking to Scott and hang up. Finally Scott turned to me. "Michelle, the phone's for you."

I reached out for the receiver. My throat began to feel as if someone had just glued it shut. In spite of my determination not to cry, I could feel my eyes beginning to well up with tears. I had thought that I just wanted to get this over with, but now I knew that wasn't true. I crossed my fingers and took a deep breath. From the corner of my eye I noticed that Scott was still standing in the hallway. He was staring at me strangely. "Go away," I whispered to him savagely.

I waited until he left before I put the receiver to my ear. "Hi, Steve, welcome home," I said in a voice that I hoped didn't sound as nervous as I felt. "What time did you get in?"

"Uh, about ten this morning," he said. "But everyone went home and unpacked, and then we all got together for dinner tonight. I'd have called you sooner, but . . ." His voice trailed off as if he couldn't think of how to finish the sentence. "Listen," he continued, "I'm just beat. We hardly got any sleep the last few nights, and we left for home early this morning." He cleared his throat nervously. "I, uh, wanted to tell you, uh, I hope you'll understand. I've really been thinking about this all the way home." He paused for a minute, and then his words came out in a rush. "I didn't mean for things to work out this way, and I know you're probably going to be pretty mad, but I need to talk to you about a change in plans for New Year's Eve."

I bit my lip. The tears that had been forming in my eyes fell silently down my cheeks. There was no hope that anything was left between us. Steve was gone. I couldn't get him back. The only thing I had left was my pride, and the least I could do was try to hold on to it. I knew just what he was going to say about New Year's Eve. Well, he wouldn't drop me. I wouldn't let it happen. I began what had to be the best acting job of my life.

"Actually, Steve," I said in a calm, level voice, "I'm really glad you brought up New Year's Eve. You see, you know how you said that we should go out over vacation. Well, I met this college guy named Don, and we hit it off really well. I made plans to be with him on New Year's Eve. So, don't worry about anything. You go right ahead and enjoy being with Heather. It's really just fine." I about choked on the next words, but I forced myself to say them. "So you see, you didn't have to be so nervous about telling me about the change in plans. In fact," I said in a burst of false friendliness, "I really hope you and Heather have as terrific a New Year's Eve as I know Don and I will."

Chapter Twelve

The silence on the other end of the phone was absolutely deafening. I'd given my send-off to Steve my best shot, and his response was absolute silence. In fact, I wasn't sure that he was even still on the phone. I was just about to hang up when Steve said, "Now you listen to me, Michelle Gunderson. You've had your say, now let me have mine." His voice was filled with a controlled fury. "I certainly can't stop you from going out with whomever you want, but I think it was pretty rude of you to accept a date with me for New Year's Eve and then break it at the last minute. You know, it's almost funny," he said, but there was no humor in his voice. "I've been so worried about you. All during the ski trip and now about New Year's, I've been afraid you'd feel left out. You see, everyone was having such a good time in Vail that they decided they all wanted to spend New Year's Eve together. I offered my house for a party, but then I felt bad. I didn't know if you'd want to be with all those people on New Year's Eve. After all, you made it pretty clear at the skating rink that you didn't like any of them. All day I put off calling you even though I really wanted to hear the sound of your voice because I was afraid that you'd be mad about the party."

I started to interrupt, but Steve cut me off. "You want to know the funniest thing of all? I finally decided that I'd call you, and if you were really mad about the party being at my house, I'd tell the gang from skiing that they'd just have to find another place for the party. You and I could do whatever you wanted for New Year's Eve." He took a deep breath, and the anger in his voice was obvious. "So I picked up the phone to call my girlfriend and tell her that I've missed her and that I hope she won't be mad about a change in plans. And I find out, in no uncertain terms, that she hasn't missed me a bit." His voice grew louder. "Well, Michelle Gunderson, you go do whatever you want, but don't you worry about me!"

"Wait, Steve, please, you don't understand," I pleaded.

Steve wouldn't listen. He cut me off. "Oh, I understand just fine now. It may ease your rotten conscience to find me a date for New Year's Eve, but I've got a big surprise for you. I won't have any trouble. Before I started going out with you, there were plenty of girls interested in me. And now that I'm not going out with you, there'll be plenty more. My ski friends and I, including Heather, will have a great time New Year's Eve. Good night and goodbye." The phone slammed in my ear.

I put the receiver back in the cradle. My hands were shaking so badly that I had to use both of them to place it correctly. I tried to comprehend what had just happened. Steve hadn't broken the date. He hadn't even thought about breaking our New Year's Eve date. I'd been the one to break it. I had to be the stupidest person in the whole world. How could I have done this to myself? How could I have done this to Steve? And more importantly, how could I straighten everything out?

Trying to think, I went to my room. I sat on my bed and nervously peeled the polish off every one of my fingernails. An hour passed, but I still couldn't figure out what to do. How could I ever make Steve believe that I didn't care anything about Don? I sat cross-legged on my bed, grabbed my brush, and began pulling it furiously through my hair. I got up and paced my room as I brushed. Finally unable to solve anything, I decided I'd just go to bed. Maybe I could hibernate for the rest of my life. But as I lay in bed, I couldn't sleep. I had to talk to Steve again. Somehow, I had to make him understand how stupid all of this was. I picked up the phone and pretended Steve was on the other end. What would I say to him? I tried the conversation about ten different ways, but none of them sounded right. Somehow I'd just have to hope the right words came to my mind when I heard his voice. Too upset to sleep, I watched my digital clock count away the minutes until it was finally morning.

I had to leave for work too early to call Steve. I decided to ask for an emergency break as soon as I got the register open and call him from a pay phone at the store. My department supervisor wasn't very happy, but she agreed to let me have the early break. I dashed downstairs to the row of black pay phones and dropped in my quarter. My hands were shaking, and as I dialed Steve's number, I almost hoped that Steve wouldn't be home so that I could just leave a message that I'd called.

The phone rang six times. I was too late. No one was home, and I could well imagine where Steve had gone. I was just about to hang up when a groggy voice answered, "Hello."

"Steve," I said, my voice shaking, "this is Michelle. Please, don't hang up on me. I have to talk to you." There was silence on the other end of the phone, so I plunged ahead. "Steve, I don't want everything to be wrong between us. I mean, I really wanted to go out with you on New Year's Eve, it's just—"

Steve cut in. "Michelle, save it. I'll survive just

fine. Really, you know, you may have even done me a favor. I called Heather last night, and she was delighted about New Year's Eve. Maybe we'll even run into you and your date. You know, Michelle, everything worked for the best, I guess. But in the future, you might want to think twice before trying to date two guys at once. It doesn't usually work."

"Just a minute." My voice rose, and the lady at the next pay phone glared at me. "I'm not trying to date two guys at once. Don isn't important."

"Right," Steve said harshly. "That's why you made a date with him for New Year's Eve. Did you tell him that I wasn't important?"

How dare he blame everything on me. "Steve," I began angrily, "I wasn't the one who took off for the whole vacation. And I never wanted us to see other people. I also wasn't the one who wanted to spend all my time with people in the ski club. You never even wrote—"

Steve sounded weary. "Look, Michelle," he interrupted, "maybe I'm just not the guy you wanted me to be. I know you don't seem like the girl I used to know. I really miss her, but she's gone. Or at least she's someplace I can't reach her anymore." His voice sounded resigned and very unyielding. "Goodbye, Michelle. Have a nice New Year's." The line went dead.

So that was it. Instead of telling Steve how much I missed him, I'd complained about what he hadn't done. Now he'd never know how I'd thought about him every day during vacation. I should have calmly explained how things had happened with Don and why. It was so ironic. If I hadn't cared so much, I could have been charming and understanding. I'd never have pushed Steve away. Well, I had, and it was too late to fix things. Heather ought to thank me. In retrospect it seemed as if I'd done everything possible to push Steve in her direction.

When I got back to ladies' sportswear, my supervisor looked at her watch pointedly. "I guess you'll be taking a short lunch hour," she snapped. I just nodded. I was afraid that if I tried to speak, I'd start crying. She pointed toward a large stack of sweaters. "Those are all to be written up as transfers to our Cinderella City store. They look similar, but many have different style numbers. Make sure you put only one style number to a transfer sheet."

The supervisor watched me pick up a pen as if she didn't quite trust me, and I couldn't say that I blamed her. Right then, my mind was about a million miles from the store, and counting inventory was the last thing I felt like doing. Worse still, I filled out one transfer sheet incorrectly, and I had to go back to get another one. She wouldn't give me a good recommendation.

At lunch I sat down at a table by myself. I'd only gotten a milk shake, and I planned to drink it quickly so that I could prove to my supervisor that I'd make up for the missed time that morning. Still, I couldn't help overhearing the conversation at the next table. Three women were talking about a security guard at the Cinderella City store who'd been hurt when a shoplifter had pulled a knife. One of the women said she'd heard the guard was one of those young college kids. In her opinion, she went on, the store ought to hire more experienced, older people. "These kids," said one of the other women, "breeze in and think they know everything in no time."

Guilt overwhelmed me. Don was at Cinderella City. What if he'd been hurt? All morning I'd tagged transfers and wished that Don had never entered my life. I kept thinking that if only I hadn't had a date with him for New Year's Eve, then maybe Steve and I could have gotten everything worked out.

I knew it was rude, but I leaned over. "Excuse me, I couldn't help overhearing your conversation. You see, I've got a good friend who works in security at Cinderella City. Do you happen to know the name of the person who was hurt or how badly?" They said they didn't know the boy's name, and one of them added, "But I'm sure if you keep eavesdropping on other people's lunchtime conversations, you'll find out eventually."

I didn't even bother to answer her. Instead I tossed my half-finished milk shake in the garbage and went down to personnel. If Jane was there, maybe she'd tell me if it had been Don who was hurt. I wasn't quite sure what I'd do if it was Don, but I felt it was important to find out. I pushed open the doors to the personnel department and looked for Jane. "I'm sorry," said a lady I'd never seen before. "Jane's gone home ill today. I'm filling in for her. Could I help you?"

I stammered about my concern that a friend of mine had been hurt at Cinderella City. The woman replied, "I'm terribly sorry, but I'm not allowed to give out that kind of information." She smiled sympathetically. "Off the record, though, I've been here about an hour and I haven't heard anything."

"Thanks," I said, feeling relieved. By the time the day was over, I was totally exhausted. I'd been on an emotional roller coaster ever since the morning. On the up side, Don was probably OK, and on the down side, what would I do without Steve? The bus bumped its way home, and I decided that I was going to talk to my mother. Maybe she could help me figure out what to do.

I walked in the house and headed for the kitchen. "Oh, Michelle, is that you?" Mom called. She came out of the kitchen wiping her hands on a dish towel. "Listen, honey, while you were at work, you got a call. Scott took this message." Mom handed me a blue scratch pad, and in Scott's barely legible scrawl I read, "Call Don, urgent." There was a phone number listed, and I hurried upstairs to my room, the number in hand.

It had been Don, I thought. *He was probably badly hurt and I spent all that time worrying about myself.* I picked up the phone in my room. *Well,* I reassured myself, *at least he wasn't hurt so badly he couldn't call.*

Chapter Thirteen

The phone rang and rang. "Oh, please," I said, crossing my fingers. "I didn't mean for anything to happen to Don."

Finally an out-of-breath voice on the other end said, "Hello."

"Don?"

"Michelle, I'm so glad you called. Let me just catch my breath; I was outside when the phone rang."

There was an agonizing wait while he caught his breath. Finally I couldn't wait any longer. "Are you OK?" I implored.

He laughed. "Sure, I'm just a little out of breath."

"But what about the stabbing?"

"What stabbing?" Don asked, confused.

I told him what I'd overheard at lunch. "So when they said it happened at Cinderella City, and it was a college kid, I thought it might be—"

"Oh, Michelle," Don cut in, "that's really sweet, but as far as I know, everyone in security is just fine. You wouldn't believe some of the stories that have gone around. Last summer a woman came into one of the stores with a garment bag and took a coat. As if that wasn't bad enough, people added to the story until they were saying that the woman had stolen six coats!"

I sighed deeply with relief. "Well, I'm glad you're OK. So what's up? My brother left a note saying that your call was urgent."

"Oh, yeah, right." There was a change in Don's voice. I could sense his hesitation. He said that he didn't mean to scare me but that he'd wanted to make sure he could get hold of me. "Michelle, remember how I've been telling you that my finances are practically zero?" He paused, and then he went on to explain that he'd counted on Christmas transportation being pretty cheap. He'd been able to afford the trip back to Denver by putting his name on the ride board at school. He was able to find a guy who was going all the way to Denver and wanted to split gas costs. "I planned to drive back and forth to school with him. Then last week he called and said he wasn't going back to UCLA; he was transferring to a school here in Colorado. That left me with no choice but to book a plane reservation, which will cost me an unexpected hundred and fifty dollars. On an already overloaded budget, that's a lot."

I could figure out what was coming next. Don was trying to tell me that he didn't have enough money to do anything very exciting on New Year's Eve. At that point I didn't care. I just didn't want to spend the evening all alone thinking about Steve. If Don just came over, it would be OK. He was interesting and funny, and he'd help me get through the evening without my going to pieces. In a sense I was glad we wouldn't be going out and making a big evening of it. I wouldn't have to pretend so hard. Right now, what I most needed was a friend, and at least Don was that.

"Listen," I said. "Don't worry. We don't have to do anything special on New Year's Eve. In fact, why don't you just come over?"

There was an awkward silence. "Michelle, you don't understand. You see, yesterday I was talking with this guy at work who's a stock boy, and he said his friend was driving back to UCLA tomorrow. I called the friend, explained my situation, and told him I'd share expenses if he had room for me. He said OK."

"But tomorrow's New Year's Eve," I said dumbly.

"I know. I feel like a total jerk, I really do. But I'll save a hundred and fifty dollars if I leave tomorrow, and that's a lot of money. I hope you'll understand." Never serious for long, Don asked,

"Will my favorite supersleuth give me a second chance this summer?"

I didn't answer his question. Instead, I said, "Don, I understand. Have a great semester at school."

Don seemed very relieved. "Michelle, you're really a terrific girl. It was great to meet you."

The line went dead. My head was spinning. Don, who I thought was this sensitive, caring friend, had dismissed me. I'd sent Steve, who really had cared, flying right into Heather's arms. I hung up the phone and began to laugh. I couldn't cry anymore; I was all cried out. What else could go wrong? The only positive thing in my life was that no other boys had asked me out, so no one else was left to dump me.

At dinner I pushed the food around my plate. There was no way I could eat, especially when the conversation turned to New Year's Eve. Mom asked innocently, "What are you and Steve doing tomorrow night?"

I looked down at my peas. "Nothing, We, uh, decided not to go out together any more."

"Oh, geez," exclaimed Scott in disgust. "You really are dumb. You'll never find another neato guy like Steve."

Mom fixed Scott with an angry look. Then she turned to me with concern. It seemed that she and Dad had been invited to a party. Thinking I was going out, too, they'd made plans for Scott to go over to a friend's house. "I hate to think of you here all alone, Michelle. Dad and I could skip the party. Or maybe Scott and his friend could spend the night here."

"No way, Mom," said Scott. I had to agree. Having two ten-year-old boys in the house wasn't going to improve my New Year's Eve one bit. In a way I wished my parents were going to be home, but at sixteen I was too old to ask Mommy and Daddy to stay home with their little girl.

"I'll be fine," I said with false cheeriness. "Really. Don't worry about me. I can stay here by myself."

My mother urged me to see if I could find someone else who didn't have a date to come over. Of course, I had no intention of really looking. At least I could let Steve think I had a date. He didn't have to know that I'd been dumped and was madly dashing around trying to find a friend to spend New Year's Eve with.

As dinner ended Mom said that she wanted me to help her with the dishes, and once Scott had left the room, she said, "Want to tell me what's the matter?"

We stood in the kitchen for the next hour while I poured out the whole story. "So you see, I've blown everything. It was my fault."

We talked a while longer, but Mom couldn't give me any answers. "Oh, honey," she said, "I can't solve your problems for you. But I do understand how much you're hurting."

I looked at her doubtfully. Seeing my look, she thought for a moment and said, "Michelle, I remember when I was just about your age, I liked a boy named Jeff Jennings. The first time he asked me out, I was so happy I thought I'd burst. In those days when a boy liked you a lot, he gave you his class ring, and you went steady. I wore Jeff's ring on a chain around my neck and thought the world was perfect."

Mom stared off into space, lost in thought. I tried to imagine her with someone other than Dad, but I couldn't. "Go ahead," I urged. "Then what happened?"

Mom sighed. "Jeff had the lead in the school play. I can't even remember what it was, but I do remember that he was going to have to kiss the female lead. I was so upset. She was this adorable girl with long red hair. And I was sure that as soon as he kissed her, he'd never care about me again." Mom shook her head. "I begged him to ask the drama teacher to rewrite that scene; I threatened to break up with him forever if he didn't drop out of the play. He kept trying to explain that the kiss didn't mean a thing, that it was just a stage kiss and it didn't matter. But I couldn't believe that, so I kept arguing with him about the scene. Finally one night after we'd been through the whole thing again, Jeff looked at me and asked for his ring back. He said that he'd been thinking about it long and hard. The stage kiss really didn't matter to him. But if I couldn't trust him and believe him, then, he said, I didn't really know him. Jeff left, and I remember sitting in my room thinking that, just as I'd predicted, the play had come between us. But the more I thought about Jeff's words, the more I realized that neither the play nor the red-haired girl had been responsible for our breaking up. I had done that myself."

The next day I arrived at Klausner's with Mom's story still fresh in my mind. It would be my last day of work. The store was filled with the chatter of excited shoppers picking up last-minute items for New Year's Eve. One girl tried on a number of cashmere sweaters before finally asking me to help her decide. "It's so important," she explained. "I just know my boyfriend's going to ask me to marry him tonight. I want to make sure I look just right." Together we picked out a soft, rose-colored sweater. She thanked me quickly before hurrying off to get new lipstick to go with it.

Everyone seemed so excited and ready for the evening that I felt more depressed than ever. The store was closing early because of the holiday, and all the employees were leaving at the same time. On my way out I stopped by personnel to say goodbye to Jane. "You've done a great job, Michelle. I've tagged your folder that you'd really like a security position, but don't rule out sales. You're better at it than you think." Then she added, "We'll call you when it gets closer to summer."

I waited by the employee exit to say goodbye to Ann and Millie from toys and Mr. Holden from ski accessories. Everyone seemed full of the excitement of a new beginning and new year, but for me there was only an ending.

When I got home there was a flurry of activity in the house. Scott was rushing around to make sure he had all the stuff he'd need for his New Year's celebration with his friend Tim. Mom and Dad were both dressing. The party they were going to was a fairly dressy one, and Mom had swept her blond hair into a french roll. She was wearing a shocking pink silk dress, and I thought she looked beautiful. She was still fussing over me saying that she really hated to leave me, asking if I was sure that there was no one I could be with that night. She posted the number where they'd be by the phone and squeezed my hand before she left. "If you get lonely, call and we'll come home."

"I'll be fine," I said, lying and watching them leave. They made a handsome couple, and I was proud that they were my parents. I wondered if anyone would ever look at me as adoringly as my father looked at my mother.

The car pulled away, then there was silence. It was an overpowering, overwhelming soundlessness. I had decided that I'd never make it through the evening unless I could convince myself that this was just another night. It was not New Year's Eve, the biggest, most important date night of the year. I picked up a mystery that I'd been wanting to read and turned on the radio. After moving the selector up and down the entire dial, I turned the radio off in disgust. Stupid DJs couldn't think of anything to talk about except that it was New Year's Eve. Unable to concentrate on the book, I put it down and turned on the TV. The noise blared in the background, but the shows were all centered on people having a wonderful time on New Year's Eve. I had never felt so lonely in my entire life. It hadn't even been this bad when we'd moved from Tucson and I hadn't known a single person in all of Denver.

Finally I gave up trying to pretend things weren't that bad. I turned off the television and went upstairs to my room. Sitting cross-legged on my bed, I tried again to really think this thing through. I went through everything that had happened between Steve and me. Before he left he'd been acting aloof. He had also been the one to suggest that we go out and do things while we were separated. Score two for my side. Still he'd never once said that he wanted us to break up. He had even taken me to the roller-skating party when hardly anyone else had brought a date. Instead of making him feel good about it, I'd made him feel miserable. Score three for his side.

In my mind I made a whole list of points in his favor and points in my favor. He'd never really said that he wanted to be with Heather while he was skiing; he'd just insisted that I go out and have fun while he was gone. I decided that that meant he had planned to spend his time with Heather. He'd also never even written me a postcard. Of course, I hadn't written to him, either.

I must have sat there thinking for at least an hour. Mom's story made sense now. I knew what she was trying to tell me. I hadn't trusted Steve. If there was no trust, then there could be no relationship. People who really cared about each other had to have faith in each other.

The telephone rang, and my heart began to pound. Steve was calling: he wanted to be with me. Somehow he'd found out that I was home and that I didn't have a date. I looked at the clock as I picked up the receiver. It was only eleven. We could still be together for the New Year.

"Hi!" I exclaimed into the receiver. "I'm so glad you called!"

"Honey," my mother said, "here I was worried that you might be feeling kind of down, and you sound just fine. Dad and I love you. Have a Happy New Year. We'll be home later."

I hung up the phone. Steve wasn't going to call after all. This wasn't a fairy tale, it was just ordinary life. And the simple fact was that Steve was out with Heather Lance. The clock edged toward midnight. Soon Steve would be kissing Heather Happy New Year. The clock ticked on.

Chapter Fourteen

When I awoke the next morning, Mom and Dad were still asleep. Scott hadn't come home from his friend's, and the quiet of the house was nerve-racking. The thought of sitting there alone was more than I could bear. Throwing on my oldest pair of jeans and a grubby sweat shirt, I decided to go for a walk. Maybe the physical activity would help me clear my head. I didn't bother with makeup, and I brushed my hair carelessly because I was sure that everyone else was still sleeping after a late New Year's Eve celebration.

Grabbing my old parka and a pair of mismatched mittens, I slipped downstairs and quietly closed the door behind me. Both the day and my mood were a matching shade of gray. I shivered, but whether it was from loneliness or the unfriendly breeze, I wasn't sure. It didn't matter anyway. I strode purposefully down the front steps, intending to walk until I was exhausted.

As I rounded the big leafless oak tree by the street, I was sure I had seen a familiar face from the corner of my eye. *Good, Michelle,* I told myself. *Now you're going to imagine that you see Steve behind every bush, tree, and pillar.* I knew he really wasn't there, but I couldn't help myself. *I'll just turn around and look very quickly,* I rationalized.

I walked toward the tree and saw Steve leaning against it. He was even wearing the ski sweater I'd bought him for Christmas under his jacket. I approached him tentatively, stopping about three feet away. "Hi," I said uncertainly.

"Hi," he replied. And we stared at each other until he said, "Uh, what are you doing?"

"Going for a walk," I answered, wondering what he was doing there.

"Oh. Want company?"

"Sure," I said, hardly believing what was happening. We began to walk side by side, neither of us saying anything. Finally I couldn't stand it any more. "Steve," I asked, "how did you happen to be out in front this morning?"

He wouldn't look at me. "I was trying to get up enough nerve to ring your door bell."

"You were?" I asked, suddenly filled with hope. At that instant I made up my mind that whatever else happened, even if I made a total fool of myself, I wanted Steve to know I cared.

Unsure of what to say and feeling that I'd better say something before I lost my courage, I ended up just letting the words pop out instead of planning them. I started by telling Steve that I hadn't gone out on New Year's Eve.

"You didn't?" he said in confusion. Inside my mitten I crossed my fingers that he'd tell me he sat home, too, but he didn't, so I plunged ahead. "I should never have accepted a date with someone else in the first place. But I was so sure you'd come back from the ski trip and tell me that Heather was your girlfriend."

"Why would I do that?" Steve seemed genuinely amazed. How could I explain to him that that's just the way things worked? I was a giraffe and she was a cheerleader. She was born to pick and choose from among the Steves of the world, and I wasn't. It was only by some crazy fluke that he'd ever liked me in the first place. I couldn't say that to him, so I began by blurting out, "Well, I know you used to like each other, and Heather really acted as if she wished you guys were back together, and she's so pretty, and you were going skiing together, and you seemed so, well, so strained around me before you left, and then you didn't even write, and—" I stopped. I was rambling, and I knew it. Looking up into those perfect blue eyes of his, I said, "Steve, I don't know how to explain it. Do you understand at all?"

Ignoring my question, he asked one of his own. "Tell me about this college guy that you

133

didn't go out with last night." I told him the truth. When I finished, Steve stopped abruptly and turned to face me. "You know what?" he said softly. "I'm a real jerk." He took my hand, and our eyes met. "Michelle, I think we need to straighten a few things out."

We walked on, hand in hand, and talked. "Remember that night at Hamburger Hamlet when I first showed you the letter from my grandmother?" I nodded. "Well, I could tell even while you were reading it that you were upset, and I felt bad. I just wanted to share my excitement with you, but I felt that if I talked about it, it'd be rubbing it in that I was going."

"But"—my voice came out in almost a whisper—"you started staying away from me even before you left. You seemed so distant."

Steve said, "I didn't know what else to do. I really wanted to be with you before I left, but when I took you to the skating party, you acted as if you hated everyone there. I figured you must really resent my going on the ski trip. I couldn't lie and pretend I wasn't excited, so I decided that the only fair thing for me to do was stay away and not make you feel any worse."

I could hardly believe what I was hearing. "The last night before you left—" I started to say.

"Go ahead," commanded Steve. "We've got to get all this straightened out."

"Well, you told me . . . Well, when a guy likes a

girl, he shouldn't just tell her to go out and have fun with other people."

"Hey," protested Steve, "that was hard on me, too. I only did it because Heather convinced me that if I really cared about you, it was the only decent thing to do."

"Heather—" The word hung in the air.

"Ah, Heather. Believe it or not, at one point I really did think she had your best interests at heart. But you're right, she's still playing her games. She's not the one for me, and I've made that very clear to her. In fact, I spent all of last night asking her where she thought you and that college guy might be and if you could really get to like him so much in such a short time."

The sun began to peak through the corner of one cloud, and the wind died down. Steve and I suddenly realized that we had covered a mile without even noticing it. Suddenly Steve stopped. As he turned me toward him, I asked, "What are you doing?"

"Kissing my girl Happy New Year." He bent, and our lips met in a kiss that immediately erased every unhappy memory of the past weeks. When we parted, I felt all tingly. Everything was going to be fine.

"You know," I said, "I've got the perfect New Year's resolution for both of us."

"Oh, yeah, what?"

I grabbed a long, thin stick and ran over to an untouched patch of snow. "Come here," I said.

"I'll show you." Steve walked over and put his arm around me as I wrote. His eyes began to twinkle, and he grinned when the words "Trust Each Other" were completed in the snow.

"That," he said, "is the best idea for the New Year." I leaned my head against his shoulder and smiled, knowing that a terrific year lay ahead.

We hope you enjoyed reading this book. Some of the titles currently available in the Sweet Dreams series are listed on page two. They are all available at your local bookshop or newsagent, though should you find any difficulty in obtaining the books you would like, you can order direct from the publisher, at the address below. Also, if you would like to know more about the series, or would simply like to tell us what you think of the series, write to:

Kim Prior,
Sweet Dreams,
Transworld Publishers Limited,
61–63 Uxbridge Road,
Ealing, London W5 5SA.

To order books, please list the title(s) you would like, and send together with your name and address, and a cheque or postal order made payable to TRANSWORLD PUBLISHERS LIMITED. Please allow cost of book(s) plus 50p for postage and packing on orders up to a value of £5.00; orders to a value of more than £5.00 are sent post and packing free. Please note that payment must be made in pounds sterling: Irish currency is not acceptable.

(The above applies to readers in the UK and Ireland only.)

If you live in Australia or New Zealand, and would like more information about the series, please write to:

Sally Porter,
Sweet Dreams,
Transworld Publishers (Aust.)
 Pty. Ltd.
15-23 Helles Avenue,
Moorebank,
NSW 2170,
AUSTRALIA.

Kiri Martin,
Sweet Dreams,
c/o Corgi & Bantam Books
 New Zealand,
Cnr. Moselle and Waipareira Avenues,
Henderson,
Auckland,
NEW ZEALAND.

If you enjoy Sweet Dreams, there's a whole series of books you'll like just as much!

SWEET VALLEY HIGH

Created by Francine Pascal
Written by Kate William

SWEET VALLEY HIGH is a great series of books about identical twins, Elizabeth and Jessica Wakefield, and all their friends at Sweet Valley High. The twins are popular, daring and smart – but Jessica is always scheming and plotting in ways only she knows how, leaving Elizabeth to sort out the mess!

Every story is an exciting insight into the lives of the Sweet Valley High 'gang' – and every one ends on a gripping cliffhanger!

So come and join the Wakefield twins and share in their many adventures!

Here's a list of all the Sweet Valley High titles currently available in the shops: